T0376222

The brave man is not he who does not feel
afraid, but he who conquers that fear.

—Nelson Mandela

MYSTERIES *of* BLACKBERRY VALLEY

Where There's Smoke
The Key Question
Seeds of Suspicion
A Likely Story
Out of the Depths

MYSTERIES *of* BLACKBERRY VALLEY

Out of the Depths

BETH ADAMS

Mysteries of Blackberry Valley is a trademark of Guideposts.

Published by Guideposts
100 Reserve Road, Suite E200
Danbury, CT 06810
Guideposts.org

Cover and interior design by Müllerhaus
Cover illustration by Bob Kayganich at Illustration Online LLC.
Typeset by Aptara, Inc.

ISBN 978-1-961442-75-7 (hardcover)
ISBN 978-1-961442-76-4 (softcover)
ISBN 978-1-961442-77-1 (epub)

Printed and bound in the United States of America
$PrintCode

Out of the Depths

Chapter One

Hannah Prentiss was peeling a butternut squash in the kitchen of the Hot Spot when her phone rang from her pocket. Hands covered in squash, she was just a few satisfying strips away from being done peeling it. She let the call go to voicemail.

But when it immediately rang again, she sighed and set the squash and peeler on the cutting board. It had been a chilly October so far, and the butternut squash soup—topped with fried croutons and a drizzle of cream and olive oil—had been a big hit, but it sure did mean a lot of peeling and chopping. She still had at least half a dozen left to go.

"I'll finish this in a moment," she told Jacob Forrest, the head chef at the Hot Spot, who was busy seasoning chicken for the chicken marsala special. She quickly washed and dried her hands then pulled her phone out of the back pocket of her jeans.

It was her best friend, Lacy Minyard. Lacy usually texted, so the fact that she'd called Hannah twice meant something was wrong. "Hi. What's going on?"

"Have you heard from Ryder?" It sounded like Lacy was in a car, judging by the soft clicking sound of a turn signal in the background.

"Ryder?" Hannah and her cousin were friendly, but they weren't in the habit of checking in with each other regularly. "No. Why?"

"When I was coming home from town about an hour ago, I saw his car parked at the edge of the woods, right by the path that leads to the entrance to McLeod Cave. He goes there sometimes, so I didn't think anything of it. But then a few minutes ago, I saw a fire truck, an ambulance, and a police car speeding by. They pulled into the parking area where Ryder's car was. The cave entrance is the only thing down that way, so I was afraid—well, I just wanted to see if you knew what was going on."

"No." Hannah got a sinking feeling in the pit of her stomach. Lacy lived on a farm outside of Blackberry Valley, and her land held an entrance to one of the many caves that threaded underground throughout the area. Many people, including Ryder, liked to explore that particular cave, which was said to be filled with interesting rock formations and underground rivers, but it was also notoriously dangerous.

There had been plenty of stories over the years. People sometimes got turned around inside the cave, or were trapped in a tiny space they couldn't get out of, or portions of the cave walls collapsed on people. All kinds of things had happened that led to people needing to be rescued. People had even died in the cave, including one of Hannah's relatives many years before.

Hannah and her brother, Drew, had always been forbidden from venturing inside, though it wasn't exactly a temptation for Hannah, who could never get past the claustrophobia she felt in small spaces. Add to that the danger and the possibility of creepy-crawlies, and she had no interest. But Ryder, for reasons Hannah would never understand, was an active spelunker who spent a lot of time exploring and mapping the caverns around the area. Had he been exploring and gotten into trouble at last?

"It can't be good, can it?" Hannah asked. A fleet of emergency rescue vehicles wouldn't be rushing to the cave entrance unless something bad had happened.

"I'm headed there now," Lacy said. "I'll be there in a second. I can let you know what I find out."

"I'm on my way." If something terrible had happened to Ryder, Hannah wanted to hear it firsthand. "I'll see you in a few minutes." She hung up and started to untie her apron. "Will you be okay if I run out for a moment?" she asked Jacob.

"I'll be fine. It's all under control."

Hannah was grateful to have such a capable chef at the helm. He would have to peel and chop the squash himself, but he could handle that and more.

She pulled her apron over her head and hung it up, grabbed her purse, and hurried out through the dining room of the old firehouse she'd transformed into a farm-to-table restaurant.

"I'm running out for a bit," she called to Raquel Holden, one of her servers, who was sliding the printout with the night's specials into the table tents.

"No problem." Raquel barely looked up. "We'll be ready to open on time."

Dylan Bowman, Hannah's other server, was seated at one of the tables, rolling bundles of cutlery in the cloth napkins. Hannah noticed that he had two forks and no spoon in the bundle he was working on.

"Check that one again," she called before dashing out the door.

She really was lucky to have found such a capable and reliable staff. Aside from Dylan—who made more mistakes than he probably should but was likeable enough that she couldn't bring herself to replace him—she had no qualms about leaving her restaurant in their hands. Raquel and hostess Elaine Wilby would double-check Dylan's work.

Hannah hopped into her Subaru Outback and headed down Main Street, driving past the brick storefronts and cafés that lined the quaint downtown, past the old Victorian homes and lush lawns of the residential area, then out of the main part of town, where she was surrounded by open fields on both sides. Along the road, trees blazed in shades of fiery orange and red and gold, and behind the fence on the left side, chestnut-colored horses stood in the shade of a redbud tree. She would never get over how beautiful Blackberry Valley was. After years of living in California, she had returned to central Kentucky where she'd grown up, and had developed a new appreciation for its beauty.

Bluegrass Hollow Farm, which Lacy's family had owned for generations, was a few miles out of town. Hannah passed Lacy and Neil's white farmhouse and kept driving. She turned onto a dirt side road and followed it along the creek until she saw the police cars and fire truck parked under a grove of trees. She parked behind Lacy's pickup and stepped out.

The first person she saw was her cousin Ryder talking to twin deputies Alex and Jacky Holt. Ryder wore tan overalls that were covered in dust and a helmet with a light on the front. He gestured wildly, though Hannah couldn't tell what he was trying to convey. Whatever it was, he was excited.

Colt Walker, a firefighter on the Blackberry Valley squad, stood next to him, also wearing dusty overalls and a helmet. Two EMTs stood in the shade beside an ambulance, looking down at their phones. She let out a breath. Ryder was okay.

"Hey." Lacy joined Hannah and gave her a hug. "He's fine, obviously."

"I'm so glad." Hannah looked around at the small crowd gathered in the shade of the redbud trees. In addition to the police deputies and the EMTs, she saw Liam Berthold, the fire chief, and another firefighter standing by the fire truck, its swirling lights casting an eerie glow over the shaded area. "But what happened?" She gestured at the emergency personnel. "Why are they all here?"

"From what I understand, Ryder and Colt found something in the cave," Lacy said. "They made it into a section that hasn't been mapped because rockfall closed it off, but they found another way in, and they saw something inside."

"What was it?"

"I don't know. No one's told me any—"

"Hannah." Ryder waved her over. "You'll never believe what we found."

Hannah pulled Lacy toward her cousin then released her and hugged Ryder.

He chuckled. "Well, hello to you too, Hannah. What's that for?"

She let him go. "When Lacy called, I thought something terrible had happened to you down there."

"No such luck." Ryder had the same dark hair and brown eyes as his dad, Hannah's uncle Gordon. He was tall, and he had always been athletic and adventurous. When he wasn't working at his job as an actuary, he was out caving, backcountry camping, ice climbing, or doing some other life-threatening sport for thrills. "But we found Uncle Chuck."

"Uncle Chuck?"

"Dad and Uncle Gabriel's uncle. The one who went missing all those years ago."

"What?" Hannah was amazed. Uncle Chuck had disappeared back when her dad and Uncle Gordon were very young. He'd gone exploring in the McLeod Cave one day, as he often did. But this time, he never came out. When rescuers went in to try to find him after his wife reported him missing, they found that one of the walls of the cave had collapsed. It was pretty clear he was trapped behind the fallen rock, but after the collapse that section of the cave was too treacherous to pass, and rescuers never managed to get to him. He'd been down there all this time.

If Ryder and Colt had found his remains, that would explain what all the emergency vehicles were about. The firemen were trained to perform tricky emergency rescues, which probably meant they'd spent plenty of time rescuing people from caves. The police were there to ensure things ran smoothly, keep the public back, and lend extra hands where necessary. The paramedics would provide first aid. Though Hannah wasn't sure what good emergency rescue or the paramedics could do for Uncle Chuck at this point. He'd been down there for decades.

"Well, not *him* exactly," Ryder said. "But proof that he was there at some point. We found his things. Hannah, he didn't die in that cave after all!" Ryder was talking so fast and with so much excitement, Hannah had trouble following.

"How do you know that?"

"We found some things that appear to have been left in the cave by your great-uncle," Colt said. "Some things that it seems might've been left on purpose when he disappeared."

"He didn't die down there, Hannah," Ryder insisted. "I mean, all our lives, we've been told the caves aren't safe because our dads' uncle died in one. Can you imagine how surprised Dad and Uncle Gabriel are going to be? Great-Aunt Minnie is gone, of course, but Nana—she'll be so happy to find out after all this time that her brother didn't die in the cave after all."

She could understand why Ryder was so excited. "What exactly did you find down there?"

"We found his things in a neat stack, just sitting there," Ryder said. "We found clothes along with his wallet, a note, a map, and a receipt."

"But if you found his things, doesn't that mean he was there but *didn't* make it out?" Hannah asked.

"No, Hannah. It wasn't like that. They weren't strewn all over. He left them on purpose." Ryder showed her a photo on his phone—clothes, papers, and a wallet in a tidy pile on the floor of a small, dark, rock-lined cavern. "See how he folded the clothes? Then there's a map, also folded, and that's his wallet with his ID inside. The receipt is for a bus ticket. He left it all there and walked away."

Hannah stared at the photo. Ryder was right. That was no haphazard pile. These weren't things left by a man trapped in a cave, clinging to life. This was a neat and deliberate pile. She couldn't believe it.

"Where are they?" She looked around for the items, wanting to examine them herself.

"Oh, they're still in the cave," Ryder said. "We left them there."

It took a moment for Hannah to absorb his words. "You did? Why?"

"We weren't sure what to do," Colt volunteered. "We didn't want to mess with the stuff, so we left it pretty much the way we found it so the police could see it, in case it's a crime scene."

"But we can lead you guys down there," Ryder said to the deputies, who were standing nearby. "We can show you exactly where we found them."

"Sure," Jacky agreed. She apparently had no qualms about underground exploration.

Alex scuffed the toe of his boot in the dirt and cleared his throat. "If you're telling me your uncle left his things there on purpose, then it's probably not a crime scene."

"We don't know for sure that's what he did," Colt said.

"In any case, his things are still inside the cave, and we need to see them to know for sure," Jacky said. "Which means we need to go in and get them."

"We don't all need to go," Alex said. "Maybe Ryder and Colt can go get them."

"You know as well as I do that stuff is potential evidence, which means you and I have to be the ones who handle it from now on," Jacky reminded her brother. "We're the police, remember?"

"It's getting pretty late," Alex said, gesturing at the darkening sky. The October days were certainly getting shorter, and the sun was low in the sky. "Maybe it'd be better to wait until tomorrow."

"You know it's dark inside caves, no matter what time it is, right?" Jacky laughed. "I'm tempted to keep going just to see what other excuses you come up with, but we don't have time for that."

She grinned at Hannah. "My brother is claustrophobic. Makes him lots of fun for adventures like this. I'll see if Liam wants to go instead. He likes caves." She called to the fire chief and beckoned him over.

Liam headed toward the group. He wore a long-sleeved shirt and jeans, and Hannah thought how nice he looked in them. "What's up?"

"These guys found evidence relating to a missing person, but they left it inside the cave like knuckleheads."

"We thought it might be a crime scene," Ryder protested.

"I'm teasing. You did the right thing. But we need to go in and bring it out, and my brother is too scared to go." Jacky turned to Liam. "You're not afraid, are you?"

Liam shook his head. "I have a lot of experience in McLeod Cave. I don't think I've ever been in the part where you guys found evidence though. I've never seen anything like that down there."

"We'd never been there either," Ryder said. "I don't think anyone has since Uncle Chuck. The entrance he used was closed off by rockfall. That's how he got trapped in there, or so the story went. But we found a small opening coming in from the other direction and rappelled into it. It's kind of a scary descent, and I don't think most people would have tried it. I mean, obviously no one has, or they would have found that stuff."

"Definitely not doing that," Alex said.

"No problem. Let me grab my gear." Liam looked around at the gathered group. "Anyone else want to go?"

Hannah considered it, imagining Liam's strong arms guiding her down the chambers of the cave. But reality quickly set in as she remembered caves were dark, filled with narrow passages, bugs, and the potential for rockfall that could leave a person trapped underground. She'd been to several of the commercial caves in the area, with their big caverns and stairs and lights, but she knew McLeod Cave wasn't like that.

"A small opening you have to rappel down to get inside a cave is not my idea of a good time," Lacy said.

"Especially one with a 'scary descent,'" Hannah added. "No thank you."

"Suit yourself," Jacky said, shrugging. "Liam, you got an extra headlamp in that truck?"

"Caving is not for everyone," Liam said kindly. He trotted to the fire truck.

A few minutes later, Jacky and Liam sported helmets with headlamps and Liam shouldered a backpack full of gear. Hannah guessed it contained ropes and carabiners, but she really had no idea. She and Lacy followed Ryder and Colt to the opening of the cave.

In her mind, Hannah always saw cave entrances as perfect half-ovals of rock, with the cave itself unfurling like a hallway beyond. This opening was little more than a hole in the ground, which Liam, Jacky, Colt, and Ryder descended into, using rocks as handholds and headlamps to light their way. Alex had already gone to the police car to wait.

Hannah knew she should leave the rest of the job to the professionals and get back to the restaurant. Saturday was their busiest night, and this was peak leaf-admiring season. With the beautiful clear skies, the Hot Spot would likely be full to bursting. Her team would need her.

But she couldn't quite make herself leave. It didn't sound like the path to Uncle Chuck's things would be an easy one, and she would worry until all four of them made it back up safely. Besides, she was too curious to leave now. Had they really found clues about what had happened to Chuck?

Hannah turned to Lacy. "You don't need to stay if you have better things to do."

"Are you kidding? There's no way I'm leaving now. I can't wait to see what they bring up." Lacy gestured toward the opening. "Besides, this is all happening on our land. I don't know what the liability issues are, but I think it makes sense for me to stay, just in case."

Hannah supposed that was true. She didn't think anyone in her family had ever blamed Lacy's family for what had happened in the cave. From what she knew, people in town were grateful that Bluegrass Hollow Farm allowed locals to access the cave entrance on their land—but she could see why Lacy was worried. Maybe they should consider limiting access to the cave or sealing up the entrance. After all, this was an age when people sued first and asked questions later.

While they waited, Hannah called Elaine to let her know she wouldn't be there in time for the first seating but would make it to the restaurant as soon as she could. She and Lacy chatted with the remaining firefighters and paramedics who waited by their vehicles. Hannah saw Liam's best friend and fellow firefighter, Archer Lestrade. Every few minutes, one of their walkie-talkies would squawk, but there weren't any updates from the group below.

"Is there any way to find out what's going on down there?" Hannah asked.

"Not really," Archer told her. "At least, not with what we've got here. The rocks are pretty good at absorbing radio waves, so unless they're very near the surface, we probably won't be able to get in touch with them."

"There's no cell signal down there either," one of the paramedics added.

"So how do you know if they're okay?" Lacy asked.

Archer shrugged. "All we can do up here is trust that God will take care of them."

Hannah did trust. She wanted to believe that God would protect them. But she also knew accidents could happen.

"Besides, Liam has extensive training in cave rescues," Archer continued. "There's no one better for this."

She believed him, but she couldn't help the nagging worry anyway.

The sky turned glorious shades of orange and pink, and then, as the sun sank below the horizon, shadows gathered in the dying light.

Hannah and Lacy talked about a trip Lacy and Neil were planning for January and about a new jigsaw puzzle Lacy had ordered for October puzzle night. Lacy asked Hannah about how things were going at the restaurant. Finally, when it was fully dark and Hannah was starting to wonder if something had gone terribly wrong, there were noises from inside the cave. Voices echoed, growing louder as they neared the entrance. Everyone moved toward the opening.

The bright glow from the headlamps was visible first, stark against the dark rock. A moment later, Liam's head and shoulders emerged from the hole, a huge smile on his face.

"We got them," he announced, heaving himself out of the cave entrance. "We got Chuck's things."

"Uncle Chuck is definitely not down there," Ryder added, emerging behind Liam. "But the things he left behind make it clear that everything we thought all this time was wrong."

"It definitely looks like your uncle did not die in that cave," Liam said to Hannah. "Judging by what we found, it really does seem as if he left his things there on purpose."

But no one had seen Uncle Chuck since the day of the accident—or supposed accident.

"So then, what *did* happen to him?" Hannah asked.

Ryder shook his head. "Your guess is as good as mine," he said. "All we know is that it's not what we thought."

Chapter Two

Hannah didn't catch so much as a glimpse of the items the four explorers brought up from the cave before Alex slid them into plastic bags and set them inside the police car.

"Do you need to take those if you don't think a crime was committed?" Hannah asked.

"We'll talk to the sheriff and let you know," Alex said.

"If we don't take them now, the sheriff is sure to tell us we should have," Jacky added. "We'll have to see if there's still a case file open and what the sheriff wants us to do."

"Don't worry, I got more pictures," Ryder said. He held out his phone to Hannah, who took it and scrolled through them. He'd gotten close-ups, so now she could see that the folded clothes were brown work pants and a flannel shirt of some kind. The map seemed to be of Kentucky. Ryder had taken photos of the ID inside the wallet and what looked like a receipt for a bus ticket purchased from the station in Bowling Green.

"That was one of the craziest caverns I've ever been inside," Liam said. "I don't know how Colt and Ryder found it."

"It was wild," Jacky agreed. "That opening was barely big enough for me to squeeze through. I don't know how the three of you managed."

"Liam rappelled down that shaft like it was a walk in the park," Colt said, laughing. "I don't think I've ever seen someone so unconcerned as they plunged into a small dark hole hundreds of feet underground."

"The descent into the cavern didn't bother me," Liam said. "And once I was inside it was amazing, with those huge helictites."

"What are those?" Lacy asked.

"Helictites are a kind of stalactite that grows irregularly. They can form diagonally or even horizontally," Liam explained.

"I'm glad you asked," Hannah told her friend. "I can't even keep stalactites and stalagmites straight in my mind."

"Think of it like this," Ryder said. "Stalactites cling tightly to the ceiling, and stalagmites rise up mightily from the ground."

"I'll have to remember that," Hannah said, though she doubted she'd need the knowledge.

"Anyway, the descent was fine," Liam went on. "What bothered me was when I realized the shaft to the cave was composed of rocks that were very unstable. If I'd weighed any more, it might have collapsed."

"See what you missed?" Jacky asked, punching Alex on the arm. "You should come down with us next time."

Alex shuddered. "I'm glad you all made it out. Now that you've seen it, Jacky, does it make sense how no one found these things in all these years?"

"For sure," Jacky replied. "I honestly don't know how these knuckleheads found it. The opening they showed us was well hidden, off the main passageways. To get to where Chuck's things were, we had to rappel fifty feet down a narrow, dark hole. No one in their right mind would try it."

"As soon as we found the entrance to that cavern, I knew it wasn't on any of the maps," Ryder said. "How could I not find out what was there?"

Hannah was trying to picture all of this and having a difficult time. She'd gone on a school field trip to Mammoth Cave National Park many years before, and she understood that the caves around here were made up of many chambers linked together by tunnels and crevices. But if the chamber where Chuck's things were found was so inaccessible, how did his things end up there? "So how did Chuck find it? And how did he get out all those years ago?"

"The cavern itself is on the maps," Liam clarified. "But it's marked as inaccessible. It was closed off by rockfall around the time everyone thought Chuck was trapped down there. Now that we know he actually escaped, I don't know. I guess we have to assume it collapsed behind him on his way out."

Colt shook his head. "It's amazing to think that we're the first people in there since it was sealed off all those years ago."

Now that everyone was safe, Hannah needed to get back to town. "Thank you for calling me," she said to Lacy.

"I'm so glad everyone's okay," Lacy said, giving Hannah a hug. "Keep me posted on what the police tell you about your uncle's things. That's the craziest story."

It *was* pretty crazy, Hannah reflected as she pulled away from the parking area. Ryder had promised to let her know if the police were able to determine anything from the articles they'd brought up. The paramedics had already left, and the police car wasn't far behind her as she made her way back into town.

Hannah considered what it meant if Uncle Chuck didn't die in that cave after all. If he'd left his things there on purpose, what happened to him? If he wasn't in the cave, where did he go? Nana—Chuck's sister—had spent so much of her life thinking her brother was dead. His wife, Minnie, had passed several years before, but Hannah was pretty sure Chuck and Minnie had a son. This would change everything for him.

Hannah finally had to put her musings aside as she parked behind the Hot Spot. The Saturday dinner rush was in full swing, and she jumped into action the moment she stepped inside.

"How's it going out here?" she asked Elaine, who stood at the hostess stand by the entrance.

Raquel emerged through the swinging doors to the kitchen, a tray balanced on her arm, and Dylan was filling a pitcher of water at the drinks station. Most of the tables were occupied. Pastor Bob Dawson and his wife, Lorelai, dined with an older couple. The other man resembled Pastor Bob so strongly that Hannah was sure they were his parents. A few women from church sat together at another table. Marshall Fredericks, the food critic at *The Blackberry Valley Chronicle*, was laughing with a few guys Hannah had seen around town, and there were several two-tops filled with couples.

"Busy, as you can see," Elaine said. Judging by the number of people waiting for tables on the benches by the doors, it would be busy for a while yet. It was music to Hannah's ears. She would take busy any day. "But tables are turning over at a good clip, and no one has had to wait too long yet."

"I'm glad to hear it," Hannah said. "Anything I can do?"

"Maybe check on Dylan," Elaine said. "I've seen him take three plates back so far. I don't know if he's getting the orders wrong or the kitchen is messing them up, but that seems to be slowing things down."

"I'll see what's going on," Hannah said.

She watched as Dylan refilled a customer's water, joking with him. Hannah recognized Ron Villaruz, who was the principal of the elementary school when Hannah was a kid, with his wife, Camille, a retired doctor at the local clinic. Dylan started to pour water into the second glass and accidently knocked it over, sending water cascading across the table.

Hannah hurried over with a handful of towels and fresh napkins from the cleaning station.

"I'm so sorry about that," she said. The menus were soggy, their napkins soaked, and their silverware sat in puddles. Water had splashed onto Mr. Villaruz's pants and onto Camille's blouse.

Dylan apologized profusely as well, trying to use the sodden napkins to wipe up the mess.

At least the Villaruzes didn't seem to be upset. "It's all right," Camille assured them, taking a napkin from the stack Hannah held out. "It's not a big deal." She used the napkin to blot at her silk shirt. Hannah would need to find a way to discreetly offer to pay for dry cleaning it.

"I don't know how that happened," Dylan said.

"It's okay," Hannah told him. "I'll clean it up. It looks like one of your other tables is ready for their check."

Dylan scurried away, and Hannah helped the couple clean up as best they could. She set up fresh place settings and menus then went to the kitchen to get a plate of the special crostini appetizer, on the house.

"Dylan strikes again?" Jacob guessed as he plated salmon.

"How did you know?"

"That's the second time tonight we've had to send out something complimentary to apologize for a mistake he's made."

"Really?" *Oh dear.* "What else happened?"

"In addition to the orders he got wrong? He dropped a plate of ravioli on the way to the table."

"He didn't." Dylan was a bit clumsy on the best of days, but this was worse than usual.

"I don't know what's going on with him," Jacob said. "But it might be time to address it. It's going to eat into our profit margin to keep covering for his inexperience."

Jacob was right. The thing was, even though he was clumsy, customers really liked Dylan, with his endearing smile and his goofy personality. "I'll talk to him," she assured her chef.

The rest of the night flew by in a blur, and by the time they were ready to close, Hannah was pretty sure they'd more than made up for Dylan's blunders with the night's receipts. She knew she needed to talk to him, but she couldn't quite bring herself to bring up his mishaps. Not tonight, anyway. It was late, and they were all tired. It had been a long, strange day, and she couldn't trust herself to stay calm and collected. She would do it Tuesday, when he showed up for his next shift.

Dylan hoisted his backpack up on his shoulder, but it wasn't closed all the way, and a stack of papers and books started to fall out.

"Whoops." Elaine caught some papers and held them out to him.

"I'll take those." Dylan snatched the papers and shoved them into his backpack. Then his face reddened. "I'm sorry. These are—Thank you."

Watching the exchange, Hannah thought that Dylan seemed embarrassed—not by what had happened, but because he hadn't wanted Elaine to see what the papers were. He zipped up the backpack and slung it over his shoulder again. His cheeks were still flushed as he waved goodbye and headed for the door.

"What was on those papers?" Hannah asked as soon as he was out the door.

Elaine slipped her jacket over her shoulders. "I didn't get a good look. Whatever it was, though, he really didn't want me to see it."

Hannah reached for her own coat. She couldn't help but wonder if Dylan was hiding something, and if he was, if it was affecting his work.

"You know who wasn't trying to hide anything?" Elaine continued. "Marshall Fredericks. He only had eyes for Raquel the whole time he was here."

"He did not," Raquel said, but she smiled as she said it.

"Did too. And I'm sure it's his doing that group was here at all. Do you think those guys from his pickup league would have chosen to come to the Hot Spot after their game when they usually go get pizza? I wonder what he had to do to convince them to change things up."

"Marshall's not like that," Raquel said.

"The food is much better here than at the pizza place," Jacob added.

"The atmosphere too," Hannah said.

Elaine snorted. "This was not about the food, or the lighting, or anything else but the fact that Marshall has a huge crush on Raquel."

"He does not," Raquel protested, even as her eyes sparkled. Hannah suspected that Raquel felt the same way about Marshall, even if she wasn't ready to admit it.

"Deny it as much as you want, but we all see it," Elaine said, a smug smile on her face. "What I want to know is, why he doesn't ask you out already."

Now it was Raquel's cheeks that were flushed, and Hannah wondered if they should show her some mercy and change the subject. But Raquel didn't seem to mind Elaine's teasing. Actually, Hannah thought her young server was wondering the same thing.

They continued to banter while they gathered their things and walked out, but as Hannah locked up, her thoughts had already returned to the things Ryder and Colt had discovered in the cave earlier that afternoon.

Was Ryder right that the items were evidence that Uncle Chuck hadn't died in the cave all those years ago?

If he hadn't, where had he gone?

Bowling Green Racetrack

Race 4

Horse: Single Barrel

$1 Win/Place/Show

3 bets

Ticket cost: $3

07 June 1959

11:22 am

Chapter Three

Pastor Bob preached from Isaiah on Sunday morning, and though Hannah appreciated the message, she found her mind wandering several times throughout the service. Her gaze kept drifting to her dad and Uncle Gordon sitting together in the third pew. Did they know anything about their uncle Chuck and what happened to him? She hadn't had a chance to talk to either of them yet, but she planned to ask them after the service.

Ryder sat in the pew behind them, next to his sister, Maeve, and her husband and three kids. Hannah sat next to her brother, Drew, and his wife, Allison, and spent much of the service watching her niece, Ava, doodle lambs and doves.

Hannah's gaze also kept drifting over to where Liam sat on the far side of the sanctuary. She knew he was brave—anyone who ran into burning buildings for a living was a hero—but after seeing him fearlessly venture into that cave yesterday, and after hearing what it was like inside, she was pretty sure he was a different kind of human altogether. She forced herself to look away and tried to stay focused on the message, but it was a challenge.

As soon as the last hymn was over, Hannah hurried over to where her dad and uncle were seated and sat down at the end of their pew. Ryder had already moved to sit on the other side of them.

"Are you going to tell them, or should I?" he asked her by way of greeting.

"Tell us what?" Uncle Gordon asked his son.

"Why doesn't this seem like good news?" Dad glanced from Ryder to Hannah and back again. He wore a cable-knit sweater over his dress shirt and slacks with a crease down the front, and he still held the morning's bulletin.

"It's good news," Hannah said. "Or, well, we think it is."

"It's not bad news," Ryder added. "We found evidence that your uncle Chuck didn't die in a cave."

"What?" Hannah's dad and uncle wore identical looks of bewilderment on their faces.

"We found his things in McLeod Cave over on the Minyard property yesterday," Ryder said.

"Things like what?" Dad asked.

"Like his wallet, including his ID," Ryder said. "On top of a neatly folded pile of clothes. And a map, and a receipt for a bus ticket."

"Are you serious?" Uncle Gordon asked, his brown eyes wide.

"Very much so," Ryder said. "It was in a cavern that was sealed off by rockfall a long time ago. Colt and I found a different way in, and his stuff was sitting there after all this time."

Dad shook his head. "But he died in that cave."

"Apparently, he didn't," Ryder said. "Or at least, we didn't find any indication that he did. Instead, we found things that make it seem like he left them behind on purpose."

"That's impossible," Uncle Gordon said. "If he didn't, where did he go?" He looked at Hannah as if she had the answer.

"We were hoping you two might have some ideas," she said.

"Us?" Dad let out a laugh. "I was a month old when he vanished. And he was barely two years old." He jerked his thumb at his brother. "We don't know anything except what we've been told, which you're now telling us isn't true."

"The person we'd need to ask is your grandmother," Uncle Gordon said. "Chuck was her brother. If anyone might know anything, it's her. Have you talked to her yet?"

"Not yet," Hannah said.

Dad looked at Uncle Gordon. "Mom and Dad are probably back from church by now, wouldn't you say?"

"Assuming they went to the early service as they usually do," Uncle Gordon said. Hannah's grandparents lived in nearby Park City, and they attended a small church in their neighborhood. "I don't know what they're up to today, but—"

"They'll be happy to see us," Dad said, pushing himself up. "Especially if we bring grandkids and news like this."

"I was looking forward to getting myself a slice of that lemon poppy seed cake Linda Weaver brought for coffee hour, but now I'm too curious to wait." Uncle Gordon used the pew in front of him to pull himself to his feet.

"Should we give them a heads-up that we're coming by, at least?" Hannah was as eager to talk to her grandparents as her dad and uncle seemed to be, but she thought it might be nice to warn them before a bunch of people showed up at their door with news that would change their world.

"How about I call them from the car?" Dad said. "Gordon and I drove together, so I'll call them while he drives us over."

Hannah looked at Ryder, who nodded. He was as anxious for answers as she was. "We'll meet you there."

Hannah pulled up to the curb at her grandparents' house, noting their car in the driveway. Ryder parked behind her and climbed out. A few minutes later, Dad and Uncle Gabriel drove up, and when they stepped out, Dad carried a box from Sweet Caroline's Bakery.

"We figured doughnuts would help this conversation go better," Uncle Gordon said.

"Doughnuts help every conversation go better," Ryder said.

"Good thinking." Hannah followed them up the walkway to the tidy light gray ranch house with white trim. The leaves on the maple tree in the yard were a fiery orange, and the yellow and crimson mums Nana had planted in the pots on the steps brightened up the porch. Dad knocked on the door.

A moment later, Nana answered the door, and her face broke into a wide smile. "Well, hello." She wore loose jeans and a T-shirt that said *It's a Great Day to Quilt.* Hannah happened to know that her grandmother felt that way about every day. "Gene, they're here. Better put some pants on."

"I am wearing pants, Elsa," Grandpa said, coming out of the kitchen and into the entry hall a moment later. "We were just cleaning up the kitchen after lunch. While wearing pants, thank you very much."

"Well, come in. It's good to see all of you." Nana ushered them in and gave each of them a hug. Hannah had seen her a few days ago, but it always felt good to be hugged by Nana. She smelled like the lemony lotion she'd always used, mixed with a hint of vanilla. "What brings you all here?" She smiled at them. "Is this an intervention of some kind?"

"No, Mom, it's not an intervention." Uncle Gordon laughed. "We're actually here to ask you about Uncle Chuck."

Her smile fell away, replaced by concern. "Chuck? Why?"

"And we brought doughnuts." Dad held out the pink box.

"I'll take those." Grandpa plucked the box from his son's hands and gestured toward the kitchen. "Come on. Let's make ourselves comfortable. I'll get plates out."

A moment later, they were all seated around the kitchen table and admiring the doughnuts. Ryder picked a Boston cream and passed the box to Hannah, who selected a maple-glazed cruller. She set the doughnut on the white Corelle plate with green flowers around the edge—the same plates Nana had used for as long as Hannah could remember.

"So what did you want to know about Chuck?" Nana asked. She bit into her chocolate-glazed doughnut.

"We've always heard that he died while exploring McLeod Cave on Bluegrass Hollow Farm," Uncle Gordon said.

"But that's all we really know," Dad added, examining his cream-filled doughnut as if to locate the ideal first bite.

"That's right," Nana said. "He was only twenty. He always loved exploring down there, and he went as often as he could. It wasn't unusual for him to be gone for several hours, but when he didn't come home one night, Minnie got worried and reported him missing. That's when they went in and found the collapsed tunnel. They tried for a long time to get through to get him out, but the rocks were unsteady and the rescuers were in too much danger, so the search was called off. By that time, he'd been trapped long enough that there wasn't much hope anyway." Nana dabbed at her mouth with a paper napkin. "That's why I never let you boys go down in those caves. They're far too dangerous."

"Why do you ask?" Grandpa cut a small bite of the half doughnut he'd taken. He was under doctor's orders to lower his blood pressure and was obviously trying to be good. "What's the sudden interest in Chuck about?"

"Well, this is going to sound crazy," Hannah said. "But do you think there's any chance he *didn't* die in that cave?"

"What?" Nana set her napkin down and gaped at them. "Why would you ask such a thing?"

"I was exploring in those caves yesterday," Ryder said. "It's really very safe, if you're smart about it."

Hannah suspected no one else at the table agreed with him.

"I really wish you wouldn't do that," Grandpa said, proving her right. Hannah could see that Nana was fighting to keep from saying something similar.

Ryder seemed unperturbed. He'd been exploring caves for most of his life, and Hannah suspected he'd heard plenty of similar warnings over the years. "Colt and I found a passage we'd never seen before, so we decided to check it out." He went on to explain how they'd encountered an opening and rappelled down, and what they found.

"You found his…things?" Nana said carefully.

"That's right." Ryder pulled out his phone, scrolled to the photos he'd taken inside the cave, and handed it to her. "The clothes are neatly folded. That's a map. That's his wallet, and his ID was inside. There's a receipt for a bus ticket in there too."

Her brow scrunched as she looked at the pictures, and then she shook her head. "Oh my." She gave the phone back to Ryder, clearly searching for words without success.

"Are you suggesting that Chuck left his things down there on purpose and simply walked away?" Grandpa asked.

"It does seem like a possibility," Dad said, "based on what Ryder found."

"But if he did that…" Nana's lower lip trembled.

"We were wondering if you could tell us anything about his disappearance," Hannah said. "None of us knows anything about it except the most basic facts."

"Or about his life in general," Uncle Gordon added. "Anything that might help explain this." He gestured at the phone.

"All right," Nana said. "But I'm going to need more coffee first." She pushed herself up and poured a cup from the glass carafe waiting on the coffeemaker. "Anyone else?"

Everyone but her husband declined. Nana poured another cup for Grandpa, and a moment later, she sat back down and seemed to be a bit more composed. She took a sip from the white and green cup and then set it on the plastic table cover.

"Chuck was always a bit wild," she said slowly. "I was only two when he was born, but I remember him being a handful even as a baby. He cried all the time, and as he grew, he always wanted to be outside running around and exploring. School was never his thing. Couldn't sit still for it, and just didn't seem to care. He struggled to control his impulses, as if whenever a whim came into his mind, he had no choice but to follow it. The only thing that he would really sit still for was music."

"Did he play an instrument?" Dad asked.

"He played lots of things, but he was an excellent fiddle player," Nana said. "Our grandfather played, and he taught Chuck when he was barely big enough to hold the fiddle. He would practice for hours at a time, even when he was supposed to be doing chores around the farm. When it was something he cared about, Chuck could focus like nothing else mattered."

Hannah nodded. That tracked with what little she knew of ADHD. "Did he love anything other than music?"

"Oh, sure. He was always going around looking at the horse farms. He loved being out in nature, camping in the woods, and exploring the caves around here. He did that a lot, much like our Ryder here. But he was truly passionate about playing the fiddle. He was performing all over town by the time he was twelve. Which, in retrospect, was probably part of the problem."

"What do you mean?" Hannah asked.

"Well, Chuck played at church sometimes, but mostly the places to play around here were bars, so he started spending time in the ones in town when he was still little more than a kid, really. And I guess they weren't as strict as they could have been with underage kids back then, because Chuck started drinking, getting into all kinds of trouble, and meeting people he shouldn't have."

"I'm surprised your parents allowed that," Grandpa said.

"They did the best they could, but I think they were distracted. Dad was never the same after the war, and Mom had to get a job down at the phone company to pay the bills. Between that and raising two kids, I'm sure they needed the money Chuck was making. But then, well, Minnie turned up pregnant."

"Minnie was his wife," Uncle Gordon said.

"She wasn't at the time," Nana said. "She was older than he was, and none of us really knew her or her family. In the end, we all came to love her, but in 1959, Chuck was barely nineteen and was forced to rush into a marriage. Mom and Dad were heartbroken. It wasn't what they wanted for him."

"Who forced them into marriage?" Ryder asked.

"Her parents, I would imagine. Maybe they weren't exactly forced, but that was how things were done back then. She got pregnant, they had a quick wedding, and six months later Roger was born."

"I always liked Roger," Uncle Gordon said, referring to his cousin who lived over in Bowling Green. Hannah had met him a few times. "He's quirky, but I like him."

"Pot, kettle," Grandpa said, sipping his coffee.

"Hey!" Uncle Gordon protested, even as he grinned.

"Roger is a nice boy," Nana said, as though said "boy" wasn't in his midsixties. "None of it was his fault, of course. And Minnie tried to get Chuck to settle down once the baby came along. But it was a struggle."

"That's a tough situation for sure," Ryder said.

"The truth is that he wasn't ready for responsibility like that," Nana said. "Emotionally, mentally, any of it. He got a job cleaning out horse stalls and whatnot over at Bluegrass Hollow Farm. Just caring for the horses at first, but then he got into training them a bit. He'd always been good with horses, and for a while, things looked like they were going to be okay. He spent his nights playing at the bars for more money and days off caving."

"He sounds like he worked hard," Hannah said.

"It must have been a lot for Minnie too, but they were making it work. He adored his son—there was no doubt about that. He talked about Roger all the time." Nana's expression sobered. "Our family should have done more to help. My parents believed he got himself into the situation, and it was his punishment to accept. As if children should ever be treated as a consequence rather than the blessing they are."

"I'm sure your parents were hurt," Grandpa said kindly. "Some of the gossip likely blamed them for the situation."

"I imagine so," Nana agreed. "I don't know. I was totally overwhelmed at the time, with one baby at home and another on the way. I was just trying to make it from one day to the next. Your father worked long hours, trying to keep food on the table. But I should have done more."

"It's hard to know how to help sometimes," Dad said.

"Especially if you're not asked," Uncle Gordon agreed.

"Well, anyway, he was in a bad place, and Minnie was pulling her hair out. Things between them were tough, from what I could tell. There was never enough money. And he always liked the horses, which didn't help."

It took Hannah a moment to figure out what she meant. "You mean he liked to *bet* on horses?"

"That's right. On payday he'd sometimes go down to the track in Franklin and squander what he'd earned. Sometimes he just went to a bookmaker in Bowling Green instead. He could place a bet there and listen to the race on the radio. It made Minnie livid, and I don't blame her. Here she was trying to feed and care for their son, and he was taking the money they needed and blowing it at the racetrack. And then, of course, he got into debt and started borrowing money to cover his losses, and it got worse from there."

"Yikes." Hannah could understand why Minnie was pulling her hair out.

"I think it got pretty bad, to be honest." She took a sip of her coffee and set the cup down thoughtfully. "And then, Chuck disappeared. Minnie called the police when he didn't come back one night, and Walter Knicely—that's your friend Lacy's grandfather, Hannah—reported that Chuck's car was parked by the McLeod Cave entrance on Bluegrass Hollow Farm. They went in and found that newly collapsed portion and figured he must be trapped behind there. They tried to rescue him for four days before they were forced to stop. My mother begged them to keep trying, but the risk was just too great."

"I went over to that section once, many years ago," Ryder said. "I could see where there used to be a rock bridge you'd have to cross to reach the entrance. Once that section collapsed, the entrance was sealed, and the bridge was inaccessible."

"So how did Chuck get out?" Hannah asked.

There was a pause. Then Ryder said, "Maybe it collapsed behind him when he left, or he knocked it down on purpose on his way out. Or maybe he found the way in and out through the top of the cavern, the way Colt and I did."

"The one with the scary descent?" Hannah said.

"That's the one." Ryder grinned. "I don't know. All I know is that from what I saw, the rescuers back in the day were lucky to have searched for four days without someone getting seriously injured."

"But what you're telling me is that he might not have been trapped behind those rocks after all," Nana said.

"I'm saying he was definitely not trapped behind those rocks," Ryder said. "We didn't find *him*, just the things he seemed to have left behind on purpose. Based on what I found in the cave, I think he walked out of there alive."

"Which begs the question, where did he go, if he wasn't trapped underground?" Grandpa asked.

"And why would he do such a thing?" Dad added.

There was a moment of silence while they all thought about this before Uncle Gordon said, "You mentioned he had gambling debts. Do you think someone he owed money to might have...?" He let his voice trail off.

"Whoa. That's dark," Ryder said.

Nana nodded. "It is dark. But possible, I suppose. I don't know all the details, of course, but I do know that one time I was over there helping Minnie with Roger when he had chicken pox, and the phone was ringing off the hook. She wouldn't answer it because she said it was just someone Chuck owed money to."

"Did she say who it was?"

"If she did, I forgot that information long ago."

"What happened to Minnie after Chuck disappeared?" Ryder asked.

"She took Roger and moved to Bowling Green. I would have stayed here to lean on the support system I had, but I suppose she didn't have one. That was our failure. Chuck was declared dead—no one even considered that he might not be—and she got remarried. We kept in touch, and from what I could tell, she made a nice life for herself. Roger turned out just fine. Married a nice girl. His kids are grown now, of course, but they're doing well."

"I haven't seen Roger in years, but I always liked him," Dad said. "And Aunt Minnie was always nice to us."

"Their house in Bowling Green had a pool," Uncle Gordon said. "That's what I remember."

"You always remember the important things," Dad said with a chuckle. "I'm glad she seems to have had a good life. She deserved one after what she went through with Uncle Chuck."

Nana took a sip of her coffee. "I suppose we'll have to tell Roger about this. That his father might not be dead after all. It will come as a shock, I'm sure."

Hannah didn't say what she suspected they were all thinking—that even if Chuck made it out of that cave alive, there was a decent chance he wasn't alive any longer. If he was twenty when he disappeared in 1960, he would be in his mideighties by now. Lots of people made it to that age, but there was no guarantee.

"Maybe it won't come as a shock to Roger though," Ryder said. "Maybe it's only a shock to us. If you're right, and he would never just walk away and leave his son behind, maybe Roger has known all along that he didn't die. Maybe he's been in contact with his father this whole time."

"Oh my." Nana blinked. "Do you think?"

"I suppose there's no way to know unless you ask him," Grandpa said.

"I have his number in my address book," Nana said. "I'll call him when we're done here."

For a moment, the only noise was the ticking of the tambour clock on the mantel. Then Hannah's dad broke the silence. "Okay, so we're saying that one possibility is that he left his things behind, came out of the cave, and had a run-in with someone he owed money to?"

"Another possibility—the more plausible one, if you ask me—is that he was planning to go somewhere," Grandpa said. "You said there was a receipt for a bus ticket in the wallet, as well as a map?"

"That's right," Ryder confirmed.

"So, the most likely conclusion is that he made a plan to go somewhere. To vanish. He left his ID behind, right?"

"It was in the wallet," Ryder said.

"It sounds to me like maybe he decided to walk away from his life as Chuck Lynch," Grandpa continued.

"From his wife? From his son?" Nana shook her head. "No. No way. There was a lot that wasn't great about his life here in Blackberry Valley. I could see him leaving much of it behind. Even though it hurts to say it, he could have walked away from me and Mom and Dad. But never his son. Chuck adored Roger. He was crazy about that kid. He might have wanted out of his own life, but he wouldn't have walked away from Roger."

Nana said it with such passion that Hannah wanted to believe her.

"Then what happened, Elsa?" Grandpa challenged gently. "Where did he go? Where has he been all this time?"

Nana didn't say anything for a minute, using her finger to trace the design of the floral tablecloth underneath the plastic cover. At last, she asked quietly, "What was the map of?"

"It was a map of this general area," Ryder said. "Kentucky and part of Tennessee, I think. Why?"

"Did it show Lexington?" she asked.

"I don't know. Probably."

"He wanted to start a horse farm," Nana said. "He was always talking about going to Lexington to start a horse farm of his own. If you're asking me what happened to him, if you're saying he left it all behind and went away on purpose, my guess is that he went to Lexington."

Lexington seemed as good a place as any to start looking. But how would they even begin? Surely he hadn't used his real name. He'd left his ID behind and, from what they'd gathered, he'd started a new life. So who was he now, and how would Hannah find him?

Chapter Four

Hannah caught up on laundry and housework on Sunday afternoon, and then she decided to see if she could find any trace of her great-uncle Chuck in Lexington before she had to leave for dinner at Drew and Allison's.

She opened her laptop and tried searching his name—Charles Lynch, Chuck Lynch, Charlie Lynch—and *Lexington.* She didn't find much of anything. The last name Lynch was common, as was the first name Charles, but none of the links she found seemed to be the right one. But just because she couldn't find him online didn't mean he wasn't out there somewhere. Lots of people in their eighties didn't have much of a digital footprint. They hadn't lived their whole lives online like her generation had. And more than likely, he wouldn't be using his real name anyway. But what name would he be using? She couldn't begin to guess.

She thought about the cave where his things had been found. Ryder and Liam had both described it, but she still couldn't really picture it. Where had the rocks fallen? Why were the rescuers unable to get to Chuck? She googled *rockfall seal off cave* and came across dozens of videos. She clicked around and realized that there were many channels made by people who explored caves with cameras and posted the footage online.

She clicked on one of them and watched as two guys who called themselves the Adventure Twins explored a cavern somewhere in Florida. Inside, the cave was dark and small, and they crawled on their bellies through narrow openings and nearly careened over ledges. They used the words *bro* and *dude* a lot and seemed to think it was funny every time they nearly died.

Hannah held her breath as they crawled over a rock bridge that cracked threateningly beneath them. She thought of Ryder and wondered why in the world anyone would do this for fun. But they clearly loved the thrill of it, and they had thousands of followers who seemed to enjoy their videos. She saw that they had dozens of videos titled things like *MOST Claustrophobic Moment of My Life!* and *We Got STUCK!* and *Crawling Through the Tightest Cave IN THE WORLD.* "No thank you," Hannah said out loud to her screen. She assumed they'd managed to make it out of those dangerous places, since they'd been around to post videos about them, but she felt nervous just reading the titles.

She did learn something interesting. She'd thought *spelunking* was the right term for exploring caves in this way, but in one of their videos, the Adventure Twins talked about how spelunkers were cavers who were unprepared and didn't know what they were doing. *Caving* was, apparently, the preferred term for people who were serious about the sport. "Cavers rescue spelunkers, bro," one of them said to the other, and they both laughed.

Hannah watched a few more videos. They were pretty repetitious, but she somehow couldn't look away, and she realized this was how content creators ended up with so many followers. But it wasn't getting her any closer to finding out what had become of Chuck, so she closed her laptop and got up to put together the salad she planned to take to Drew and Allison's. She'd just finished rinsing the spinach when the phone rang.

She glanced at the caller ID and answered. "Hi, Nana."

"I spoke with Roger," Nana said without preamble. "He was very surprised to hear that his father might have made it out of that cave alive. I'm nearly certain it was news to him."

"In that case, it must have been quite a shock," Hannah said.

"Very much so," Nana said. "Though he took it well. He had a lot of questions, naturally, so I told him you would get in touch with him."

"Why me?" Hannah hadn't seen Roger since she was a child. "Ryder was the one who found the things in the cave."

"You're the one trying to figure out what happened to Chuck, aren't you?"

Was she? She had hoped the police would work on it. Though if he'd been declared dead, then it couldn't be an open missing person's case. Would they want to look into it, if not?

But even if the police did investigate, she realized she wanted to talk to Roger. She had so many questions for him about what he'd been told about his father and what these newly uncovered clues might mean.

"I guess I am," Hannah said.

"You're so good at solving mysteries, I figured you'd be all over this one."

"I've just gotten lucky a few times."

"Don't sell yourself short, Hannah Marie. You've developed a talent for solving mysteries. And this one is a doozy. Of course you're going to investigate."

"All right, Nana." She wasn't sure what she was agreeing to, exactly. "Can you give me Roger's contact information? I'll reach out to him."

"Of course."

After she hung up, Hannah typed an email to Roger, reminding him that she was his cousin Gabriel's daughter and telling him that Nana suggested she reach out about the things Ryder found in the cave.

Hannah had just hit send when there was a knock on her door. She opened it to find Ryder holding a large clear plastic bag, which he set on the table. Through the plastic, Hannah could see dusty pants, a leather wallet, and a few pieces of paper.

"Those are the things from the cave," Hannah said.

"Jacky called a little while ago," Ryder said. "She told me Sheriff Steele has decided not to investigate this. As we thought yesterday, there's no crime if Chuck left on purpose. He was declared dead decades ago. As far as the police are concerned, that's still his official status."

"But what if he's not?"

"Then we'll need to prove it. That's why I'm bringing this stuff here. I figure if anyone can figure out what happened, it's you."

"The fact that we found evidence he didn't die like everyone thought wasn't enough to convince the sheriff?"

"I asked the same question. Jacky told me to let her know if we discovered any evidence that was pertinent to the case. Failing that, we're on our own with this one. They're strapped for resources as it is. Besides, you're already working on it, right?"

"Why does everyone keep assuming that?"

"Oh, I don't know." He grinned. "It probably has something to do with the fact that you showed up as soon as there was a hint of a puzzling situation and that you've solved several mysteries since you've been back in town. You can't tell me you're going to just let this go?"

Hannah wanted to argue but realized she couldn't, any more than she'd been able to argue with her grandmother moments before. "Fine. Yes, I'm going to try to figure out what happened to Uncle Chuck."

"Good." Ryder turned to the door. "Thanks, Hannah."

Once he left, Hannah sliced strawberries and used a peeler to shave off slivers from a block of parmesan. After she put the cheese back in the fridge, she went over to the bag on the table and examined the items through the plastic. The wallet and papers sat on top of the neatly folded clothes. They looked just as they appeared in the photos Ryder took inside the cave.

She took a deep breath then opened the plastic seal and slid the pile out.

First, she picked up the wallet. It was a simple billfold made of worn brown leather, cracked and dry.

She opened it and found a driver's license tucked into one of the two slits in the leather. She tugged gently at it, and it slid out. It was a square of thin cardstock with the words *Driver's License* printed in a blocky font at the top. *Charles Nicholas Lynch* was written in black ink on the top line, and underneath that was the address of a house over on Main Street.

There was no photo, no other identifying information. She thought about all the personal information—height, weight, eye and hair color—that was on her license now, along with all the safety features on today's licenses, and shook her head. This was so rudimentary. Still, it was a good indication that the wallet belonged to

Chuck. And that he hadn't planned on using his real name when he got wherever he was going.

There were no other cards or cash in the wallet, but there was a receipt in the bill slot as Ryder had said. She pulled it out and set it on the table.

It was indeed a receipt for a bus ticket. It was a small scrap of paper, an old-fashioned cash register receipt printed in purplish-black type with the word *Trailways*, and an address in Bowling Green. One ticket had been purchased on November 5, 1960, and though the destination was not specified, the cost was recorded as twelve dollars.

Hannah studied the receipt, hoping to find more information hiding on the scrap of paper somewhere, but if there was something more to glean from it, she didn't see it. She tried to focus on what she did know. Chuck had bought a bus ticket to somewhere. That indicated, as Ryder had said all along, that Chuck hadn't died in the cave but had planned to take a journey. Had planned to leave.

But why did he buy a bus ticket when he owned a car? The car he'd left outside the cave entrance that had drawn Walter Knicely's attention. Why did he leave his car behind? Was it so that someone would see it parked there and think he was inside the cave? If so, it worked.

She checked the wallet again, hoping to find anything that would give her a clue about what had happened to Chuck, but there was nothing else that she could see. No cash, no cards, nothing but a beat-up leather wallet.

She set it aside and reached for the map resting on top of the pile of clothing. The southern border of Indiana was visible on the panel that was facing up. She unfolded the map carefully. One side showed the outline of Kentucky, and the other side showed Tennessee. It was, she could see, a road map, showing major thoroughfares and smaller highways. She studied the Kentucky side of the map. There was Lexington, just north of the central part of the state, and Louisville, along the Indiana border. Most roads went into and out of those two cities. She also saw Bowling Green, west of Blackberry Valley, along with Richmond, Elizabethtown, Paducah, and a few other smaller cities.

She studied the area around Bowling Green. Blackberry Valley wasn't on this map, but then there weren't any major highways coming into or out of the town even now, so that was probably why. Some of the highways that currently existed weren't on the map, and Hannah assumed they hadn't been built when this map was printed. She searched the key area, looking for a date. In tiny type, she finally found the words *Copyright 1958*. So any road built after that point wouldn't be on the map.

Then she noticed something. A faint circle, drawn in pencil, around the city of Louisville. Another around Lexington, where Nana thought he might have gone.

Why did he circle those two cities? Was one of them his destination? Had Chuck been studying this map as he contemplated where to go when he disappeared? Or had he circled places to avoid? But no, that didn't make sense. Besides, there was no way to know whether he was the one who'd made the pencil marks on the map.

Where did you go, Chuck?

She studied the shape of Kentucky. There was its straight edge along the southern border, the bulbous round shape of the eastern side of the state, narrowing to a point in the west, the border meandering as it followed the Ohio River. The shape on the map didn't reveal anything about the gorgeous hills and trees or the open fields and streams.

In Hannah's mind, Kentucky was the most beautiful state in the union, but a person couldn't tell that about it by looking at a map. Nor could they tell anything about its people—warm and welcoming—or the things that made it famous, like bluegrass and horses.

Still, now she had a clue she hadn't had before. There was a chance Chuck had gone to either Louisville or Lexington. And Nana had said he'd always talked about Lexington. Hannah hadn't found any trace of him in her search, but that didn't mean he wasn't there. She would need to do more research. And she could look into Louisville as well.

She started to fold the map, but something on the Tennessee side caught her eye. She opened the map again and spread it out on the table. There was a small silvery circle around Nashville as well. Nashville was only a two-hour drive from Blackberry Valley. It probably would have taken longer back then, since it looked like the interstate hadn't been built yet. Though it was in a different state, it was still within the same general distance as Lexington and Louisville. Did Chuck consider Nashville as well? If so, which city had he chosen? Had he gone to any of them in the end?

She folded the map again and set it aside before turning her attention to the clothes. She picked up the dusty flannel work shirt. It had been brown and tan, though now it was covered in a fine grayish-brown powder. It smelled musty, and there were a few holes made by some kind of creature over the years. It was a size medium, made by a brand she'd never heard of. She couldn't find anything noteworthy about it, aside from the fact that it had been found with Uncle Chuck's things.

Beneath the shirt was a pair of brown work pants. The thick, stiff denim was also covered in a fine layer of dust and smelled musty. Why had he left these clothes behind? Surely he didn't walk out of the cave naked. He must have brought different clothes into the cave with him and changed inside. Why had he done that? Was it so he wouldn't be recognized when he came back out?

She set the clothes on the table and brushed the dust off her fingers. What did she know? She rinsed her hands then grabbed a pen and a small notebook from the kitchen drawer to jot down the thoughts as they came to her.

Uncle Chuck left a map with his things when he disappeared.

On the map, someone circled Lexington, Louisville, and Nashville.

He bought a bus ticket, and though she didn't know where the destination was, she did know that it cost him twelve dollars to get there.

He left his car behind and took a bus to wherever he went.

He left his driver's license, which would have identified him.

He changed clothes before he left.

Questions swirled through Hannah's mind. Seeing the things Chuck had left behind raised more questions than it answered. She had no idea what happened in that cave all those years ago, or where Chuck had gone, or what happened to him after that.

But she wasn't going to figure it out tonight. She needed to get going or she'd be late to Drew's house. She would work on it again in the morning.

She set the map and the wallet on top of the clothes and was sliding the whole stack back into the bag when she felt something in the pocket of the pants. Paper of some kind, or at least that was what it felt like through the stiff fabric. She gently eased two fingers into the pocket and pulled out a thin slip of paper.

It was a bill of sale from a pawn shop, dated the same day as the bus ticket receipt. It was from Goldrush Pawn there in Blackberry Valley, and showed that Chuck had sold a watch, a ring, and a pair of silver cuff links. Altogether, the sale netted him twenty-five dollars.

Hannah already believed that Uncle Chuck left his things in that cave on purpose, but this clinched it for her. This hadn't been a spur-of-the-moment decision for him. It was premeditated. He sold his valuables for cash. Enough cash to buy a bus ticket and then some. Enough to start a new life somewhere else.

After the kids were excused from the dinner table that evening, Hannah and her father told Allison and Drew about Uncle Chuck.

"So he just left his things in a cave and walked away?" Allison asked.

"That's what it seems like," Hannah said.

"And then what?" Drew asked. His sandy-blond hair was brushed back, and he'd changed from his church clothes into jeans and a V-neck sweater.

"We don't know." Dad shook his head. "I think he owed money to someone and couldn't pay up, so he faked his own death and escaped."

"How could he possibly owe someone enough money that they would threaten his life?" Drew said. "This is Kentucky, Dad. It's not like the mob's here."

"Actually, back in the fifties and sixties, the mob *was* here in Kentucky," Dad said. "Up in Newport. They had casinos and all kinds of gambling up there, and the mafia ran it all. It was Las Vegas before Las Vegas. The original Sin City."

"But the mob?" Allison scrunched up her nose. "That doesn't sound likely."

"I know it doesn't, but that doesn't mean it isn't true. The mob totally ran that town. They only got the kibosh put on 'em when they went too far in 1961, when they were caught trying to rig an election. After that, the cops shut it all down, and they mostly moved out west to Nevada, where the authorities weren't as concerned with things like legality. But back at this time, when Uncle Chuck was around, the mob very well could have been involved."

"How? Would he have gone up to Newport, to the casinos up there?" Hannah asked, turning the idea over in her mind.

"It's possible," Dad said. "If he really was into gambling, what's to say he stuck with betting on horses in Bowling Green? As you suggest, he could have gone up to Newport and messed with the wrong people."

It didn't seem like the most likely theory to Hannah, but it was a valid one. "That's an idea."

"Maybe he ran off and joined the circus," Drew said, smirking.

"Does that actually happen?" Hannah was pretty sure her brother was kidding, but she'd already been wrong about mob activity in Kentucky, so who knew? "You hear about it in stories, but does it ever actually happen in real life?"

"I don't think so," Allison said.

"Actually, it has happened," Drew said. "I had a friend in college whose grandparents met that way. His dad was an acrobat, and his grandma fell in love with him while the circus was in town. When they left to go to the next place, she went with them. She became a cook, making meals for the performers. She never went home. She literally ran away with the circus."

Okay, maybe he wasn't joking. But it didn't seem like the most plausible scenario to Hannah. "It shouldn't be that hard to find out whether there was a circus in town," she said. "I'll look into it."

"What about witness protection?" Allison suggested. "Is there any chance he got caught up in something he shouldn't have, and he had to be given a new identity and disappear?"

"That's another thing that happens in books but seldom in real life," Hannah said.

"But it definitely does happen," Dad said. "Just not as often as books make you think. It's astonishingly hard to assume a new identity, to give up everything that you know and love and start a new life. It sounds miserable."

"It does," Hannah agreed. "But that's basically what we're saying Chuck did, one way or another. Started a new life, no doubt with a new name. Maybe witness protection was involved after all."

"I don't think the program was around then," Drew said. "I saw a show about it, and from what I remember, they said it was started in the midsixties and was officially authorized in the early seventies."

"Well, never mind then," Allison said. "That won't work. But he must have gone somewhere."

"The circus," Drew said with a grin. "I'm telling you, that's it."

Hannah left that night even more confused about what had happened to Chuck, and even more determined to find out.

Chapter Five

Hannah woke on Monday morning with a plan. It was her day off, and there was plenty of work she wanted to get done—catch up on invoices, review the budget and expenses, try out a new recipe for brown butter and sage pumpkin ravioli—before heading to Lacy's monthly puzzle night.

But she already knew all of that would have to wait. She was going to use her time off today to find Chuck. She was going to figure out what had happened to him all those years ago. She was going to solve the mystery that the family hadn't even known about until two days ago.

But first, she was going to get some coffee.

She got out of bed and staggered into the kitchen to make a pot. The day had dawned gray and wet, so Hannah decided on a wool sweater and boots with her jeans. Soon, the smell of rich dark coffee filled the apartment, and she sat down at the table with her Bible and a cup of coffee. One of her readings for the day was from Psalm 130.

Out of the depths I cry to you, LORD;
Lord, hear my voice.
Let your ears be attentive
to my cry for mercy.

Feeling renewed, she fried some eggs and slathered butter on whole wheat toast. After cleaning up the dishes, she reached for her phone. It might be too early to call most people, but Lacy was a chicken farmer. She would be up.

As expected, Lacy answered on the second ring. "Hey, you. What's up?"

"Do you want to go on an adventure with me?" Hannah asked.

"What kind of adventure?"

"I thought we'd start at the library."

"Wow. You really aren't selling this whole adventure thing."

"You can explore the whole world through books."

"Okay." Lacy sounded dubious. "What else is on your adventure list?"

"Then I thought we'd try to find an old pawn shop."

"Hannah, we need to talk about your idea of adventure."

"I suspect it doesn't exist anymore, but I don't know for sure."

"Even better."

"I also thought I might stop in at the bookstore. I have an old map, and I wondered if Neil might be able to tell me anything about it."

"Now you're talking." Neil was Lacy's husband, and in addition to owning and running Legend & Key Bookstore, the local bookshop, he was really into old maps.

"So you're in?"

"I mean, I was going to scrub out the chicken coop this morning before I start cleaning the house for puzzle night, but somehow I'll try to tear myself away from that."

"I'll take it."

"At the library, you should make sure to check out a dictionary and look up the word *adventure*. You're using it wrong."

"How about I meet you at the library at nine when they open?"

"It's better than cleaning up after the chickens."

"I'll see you soon."

Hannah slid the map that had been found in the cave into a plastic zippered bag, which she slipped into her tote bag. She found Lacy waiting outside the library a few minutes after nine. Hannah had walked over—a perk of living downtown—but she saw Lacy's black pickup parked in the small lot behind the redbrick building.

"Thanks for coming," Hannah said as Lacy opened the door.

"Of course. What else would I be doing at the busiest time of the year on a farm?" Lacy joked, letting the door close behind them. "So what are we looking for?"

"I was hoping to start with the newspaper archives."

"Ah. You're after news from the time Chuck disappeared?"

"That's what I'm hoping for."

"Let's ask Evangeline where to start our search." Lacy was already headed to the front desk, where the head librarian was typing at a computer.

"Hi, Evangeline," Hannah said as they approached the desk.

She greeted them with a warm smile. "Good morning. How are you both doing today?" Evangeline's gray hair was piled in a messy topknot, and she wore a chunky cardigan over a T-shirt, with several long necklaces layered on top.

"We're good," Lacy said. "Ready for an 'adventure.'" She used her fingers to make air quotes.

"A bookish adventure is the best kind."

Lacy laughed and rolled her eyes. "I will never understand you people."

"Maybe we'll explain it to you when you're older," Evangeline teased.

"We were hoping you could help us find some old newspaper articles," Hannah said.

"Absolutely. Do you know how to access the archive?"

"I'm new to it," said Lacy.

Hannah grinned at her. "See? Even more adventure."

Lacy rolled her eyes again, and Evangeline laughed. "It's no problem. I can show you," she said. She walked out from behind the circulation desk and led them to a bank of computers set along the side wall. She pulled another chair over so there were two at one of the terminals and indicated Hannah and Lacy should sit. Then she clicked an icon on the desktop and opened a page with a dizzying array of links and buttons.

"The newspaper archive is here," Evangeline said, clicking on a link labeled *Newspaper Database*. "Here you can set your search parameters. Are you looking for local news, or do you want to search national papers as well?"

"I think local," Hannah said. "At least to start." She couldn't imagine Uncle Chuck had been national news.

"Great. There's actually a nearly complete archive of *The Blackberry Valley Chronicle* right here." Evangeline clicked on a tab on the search page. "You can enter the time frame you want to search, as well as any keywords."

"Thank you," Hannah said. "That's perfect."

"Let me know if you need any help." Evangeline bustled away.

"We will," Lacy called after her.

Hannah selected the year 1960 for the date range. She added *Chuck Lynch* as a search term. Several results came up, and she clicked on the first link. It was an article dated November 8, 1960.

Rescuers Working to Free Trapped Caver

Rescuers reported to the entrance of a cave on land owned by Walter Knicely on Sunday night after a local man went missing.

Charles "Chuck" Lynch was reported missing by his wife on Sunday afternoon when she alerted the police to her husband's disappearance nearly twenty-four hours after he was last seen leaving his job as a farmhand on Bluegrass Hollow Farm, owned by Knicely. Sunday evening, Knicely noticed that Lynch's car was still parked by the entrance to McLeod Cave. He called Mrs. Lynch, who then called the Blackberry Valley Police Station with this updated information, and emergency personnel responded to the scene.

Rescuers reported finding one of the tunnels inside the cave collapsed, likely trapping Lynch inside the cavern called the Boneyard because of its unique limestone formations. Personnel from the Blackberry Valley police and fire departments, as well as other local cavers familiar with the area, have been working to reopen the tunnel and free Lynch.

"The rocks in that area have always been loose , and it's well known that this tunnel has some spots that are susceptible to rockfall," said Brent Wallace, a member of the fire department

and an avid caver himself. "It's a very narrow passageway. You have to kind of wiggle through, and it's always been somewhat unstable. I've had a few scary moments there myself, when I thought the rock might not hold. Unfortunately, the recent collapse has made the entire area extremely dangerous. We're working as hard as we can to get Lynch out while protecting the safety of the rescuers."

McLeod Cave is a popular spot for locals to explore. Though the entrance is on private property, the cave has always remained accessible to all. "We are lucky to have such an interesting cave under our family's land, and we have always been happy to allow cavers to come in and explore," said Knicely. "We are heartbroken to hear about the accident and are praying for Chuck's safe return."

There is no word on why Lynch was in the cave or when he might be freed. It is believed he was exploring the cave alone when he became trapped.

Lacy squinted at the article. "I still don't understand why people think it sounds fun to go exploring in caves. If I'd had a close call in a narrow passageway I had to wriggle through underground, you would not find me going back for more."

"I don't understand it either," Hannah said. "But I guess there must be some appeal, since people keep doing it. I suppose it must be interesting to find caverns and tunnels no one has ever seen before. I watched some videos online, and the guys exploring the caves sounded nuts to me, but they seemed to think it was really fun to see what was down there."

"I suppose." But Lacy didn't look convinced.

Hannah thought for a minute, trying to imagine what it would be like to be trapped inside a pitch-black cave, alone, with no food or water, waiting for rescue. But then she remembered that Chuck hadn't actually been trapped behind those fallen rocks. He got out, leaving his things behind almost certainly on purpose. All that time people were risking their lives to save him, he hadn't been there at all.

"Let's see if there are any follow-up articles," Lacy said.

Hannah clicked back to the search page then opened the next link, which led to an article published a week after the first one.

Search Called Off for Missing Caver,
Questions Abound

Four days after rescuers first reported to the scene of a collapsed tunnel where caver Chuck Lynch was believed to be trapped, authorities called off the attempt. "We are heartbroken for the family of Chuck Lynch," said firefighter Brent Wallace. "But access to the area where he's trapped is becoming increasingly dangerous as more people disturb the precarious rock, and we could no longer justify risking the lives of so many rescuers in an effort to recover Lynch."

"'Recover' Lynch," Lacy said, pointing to the screen. "Not 'rescue.'"

"I suppose they thought chances of him still being alive were slim," Hannah said, shivering. So many people had risked their lives trying to save a man who wasn't in danger to begin with. "Let's see what else they say."

In the wake of the aborted recovery effort, some have asked why it took Lynch's wife almost twenty-four hours to report him missing. Asked to comment, Mrs. Lynch said, "It was unfortunately not unusual for Chuck to stay out all night. I didn't call to report him missing until after I checked in all the usual places to be sure he wasn't there." Asked what the "usual places" were, Mrs. Lynch declined to comment.

Others have asked about what led to the collapse of the tunnel that trapped Lynch in the cavern. "That area has always been treacherous," Wallace Rexham, a local caver, said. "But while it was common for sections of rock to break off as you went through, I didn't think it was about to fully collapse like it did. It's really odd." When asked what he thought happened, Rexham said, "I just wonder if something unusual caused the collapse, is all. It seems strange to me."

Others disagreed. "That section of the cave was treacherous. It always has been, and anything can happen underground," Fire Chief Patrick Berthold said. "Putting a foot or arm with too much weight in the wrong place could have caused the whole thing to cave in."

In the wake of the tragedy, questions abound about the future of access to McLeod Cave. Walter Knicely, owner of the land on which the cave entrance sits, said, "I don't know whether we're going to continue to allow folks to access the cave from our land or not. It would be a shame if we had to deny entry. So many people in this town really enjoy exploring the caverns. On the other hand, this tragedy really makes you wonder whether it's worth it. I would hate for anyone else to get trapped and lose their life in the cave."

"We know he didn't close the entrance to the cave in the end," Hannah said.

"And as far as we know, no one else has died down there," Lacy added.

"Not that anyone actually died down there to begin with," Hannah said. "They just thought he did."

"Right." Lacy chewed on her nail. Then she said, "That caver said something completely different than Liam's dad said, didn't he?"

"He did," Hannah said. "The first guy"—she checked the article again—"Rexham, he said he didn't think that could just happen. But Patrick said it could. Ordinarily, I'd put my money on Patrick being right, but we've almost come to the conclusion that Chuck staged the collapse himself and he wasn't trapped down there. It seems like this Rexham guy ended up being right."

"So you really think he caused the rockfall on purpose on his way out?" Lacy asked. "To make everyone think he was trapped inside? That's a terrible thing to do."

"So is walking out on your wife and son," Hannah said.

"I guess you're right," Lacy said. "When you put it like that, making the cave collapse to cover his tracks doesn't sound so improbable."

"We don't know if that's what happened," Hannah said, recalling her grandmother's repeated insistence that Chuck had adored his son. "Just that it's possible. Let's see what else there is." She clicked back to the search page and found a much shorter follow-up article the next week, but it didn't contain any new information. After that, the story dropped out of the newspaper altogether.

"What now?" Lacy asked.

"I want to see if I can access the vital records for Lexington. Birth, death, and marriage records."

"Do you know how to find those?"

"I've done it before," Hannah said. "Let me see." She went back to the main search page and started poking around, but she couldn't remember exactly where to find what she was after.

"Hang on. Let me go see if Evangeline can help us." Lacy hopped up and went to the circulation desk. While she was gone, Hannah read the articles again, hoping to see some clue she missed the first time through. She was just finishing the last one when Lacy returned with Evangeline in tow.

"Lacy tells me you're interested in vital records," the librarian said.

"That's right. I know you've shown me how to find that before, but I can't for the life of me remember how."

"That database is tricky to find." Evangeline took her down a relatively complicated path before the familiar screen popped up. "Here we are. Do you know what county you want to search?"

"I'm looking for Lexington."

"Fayette County then." Evangeline showed Hannah how to narrow her search parameters to particular counties.

Hannah typed *Charles Nicholas Lynch.* He probably stopped using that name when he left, but she didn't know what other name to try, and she was hoping she might have more success here than she'd had with a basic web browser. Even if he'd used a new name for everything else, it was possible he had still used his legal name for official matters. Not likely, but possible.

"Goodness. Is that the guy who died in that cave all those years ago?" Evangeline asked, her eyes wide. Then she flapped a hand. "I'm sorry. It's none of my business what you're searching for."

"It's fine." Hannah brushed off her concern. "And yes. He was my great-uncle."

"I was a child when he died, but it was a big deal in these parts, let me tell you. I remember how they searched for him for days before finally calling it off. My parents forbade me from ever going into the cave after that. Not that I ever wanted to. Just the image of him sitting trapped in that cave as time slowly ran out—well, it was enough to fuel my nightmares for years."

"It's too late to change your nightmares, but I have some news that may help." Hannah told Evangeline what they'd found.

The librarian gaped at her. "You mean he didn't die in the cave after all?"

"It would appear not. From what we can tell, he tried to make it look like he did and then left town on purpose."

"Oh wow." Evangeline shook her head. "Okay. Now I see why you're looking into vital records. You think he might have gone to Lexington?"

"My nana—his sister—said he was always talking about going up there to start a horse farm. It seems like a good place to begin our search."

"Indeed. Let's see what we can find."

Hannah hit return, and a handful of results came up. But when she clicked on them, she saw that there was only one result for a man named Charles Lynch, and he died in Fayette County in 1921.

"That's not him," Hannah said. "Neither are any of these other Charleses. Or Lynches."

"So he didn't marry, own property, or die in Fayette County," Lacy said.

"At least not under that name," Evangeline said.

"Too bad. I have no idea what other name he would have used," Hannah said.

"Let's keep looking," Lacy said. "There are plenty of other counties in Kentucky we can try."

"He also could have gone to Louisville," Harriet said. "Or possibly Nashville."

"Tennessee's vital records are under a whole different system. I'm afraid we don't have access to that," Evangeline said.

"Let's try Jefferson County then," Lacy said. "For Louisville."

Hannah adjusted the search and hit return, but they didn't find him. "Again, either he didn't go there, or he didn't use his real name when he did."

"Which would make sense if he wanted to disappear, as indicated by the fact that he left his ID behind," Lacy said. "Let's try Barren County, just to see what comes up."

Hannah ran the search for the county where Blackberry Valley was located, and she found a birth certificate for Charles Nicholas Lynch, a record of his marriage to Minerva Rebecca Shirley in 1958, and his death certificate, issued in June 1961. So it had taken a while to get his death officially on the record, but maybe it took longer when there wasn't a body. Maybe Minnie hadn't filed for it right away. But it was there. According to the state of Kentucky, Chuck was dead.

But she'd already known that. Minnie wouldn't have been allowed to get remarried without Chuck's death certificate.

"If there's anything more to learn here, I don't know what it is," Hannah said with a sigh.

"Unfortunately, I'm afraid you're right," Evangeline said. "Is there anything else I can help you find?"

Hannah supposed she should do her due diligence. "Do you know how I'd find out if there was a circus in town around this time?"

"Ooh. You think he ran away with the circus?" Lacy asked, her eyes bright.

"I don't, but Drew floated it as a theory. I'm hoping there's a way to prove him wrong."

"It'll take me some time, but I can probably dig through some old records and find out," Evangeline said. "Anything else?"

Hannah thought for a moment. "Is there any way to figure out how far you could get from Bowling Green with a bus ticket that cost twelve dollars in 1960?"

"Intriguing." Evangeline mulled over her question. "Nothing comes to mind off the top of my head, but how about I poke around a bit in the local history archives? There may be something in there, like an old bus schedule or fare schedule or something of that sort."

"That would be amazing."

"I'll see if I can find anything about Chuck or his death while I'm in there too. And if I can't find a circus advertisement or bus schedule here, I'll call over to the Bowling Green library. The head librarian there is a friend of mine."

"Thank you." Hannah loved thinking of the local librarians as a sort of network of superhero sleuths, digging through old records that would be opaque to anyone else on a quest for answers. "I appreciate it."

"Are you kidding? I love this. Going through archives is my favorite thing."

"I'm so glad people like you exist," Lacy said with a laugh. She turned to Hannah. "Anything else?"

Hannah thought for a moment. "Do you have any books about caving and spelunking?"

"Sure," Evangeline said. "Interested in taking up the sport?"

"Not in the slightest." Hannah laughed. "I want to learn more about it, to try to understand what attracts people to it, I suppose. Maybe it's not a good idea. It probably won't help with finding any answers."

"It's always a good idea to learn something new," Evangeline said. "Even if it doesn't help you find your great-uncle, what harm can it do to learn more about it? And we have quite a few books on that topic, given the number of caves in this area." She gestured for them to follow her. "Come on. I'll show you where they are."

Hannah logged out of the computer, and then they followed Evangeline past the reference area and a reading area to the long rows of nonfiction books. Evangeline ducked down an aisle, stopped, and crouched in front of one section. "The books on caving and spelunking are here." She ran her hand over a few spines. "Hopefully you can find something interesting, if not useful."

"Thank you."

Evangeline waved and headed back to the front while Hannah tugged a few books off the shelf. There was a caver's memoir. There was a book about caves in Kentucky. There was a general reference book with photographs of different formations and caving terminology. It also included the geology of caves, giving a history of how caverns formed. Hannah paged through them and then gathered them all up in her arms.

"You've got a lot of reading ahead of you." Lacy eyed the stack. She held a memoir by a blind man who had climbed Mt. Everest.

"Like Evangeline said, it doesn't hurt to learn something new."

"They'll make a spelunker of you yet," Lacy said.

"A caver, actually."

"What's the difference?"

"Cavers take themselves very seriously, from what I understand."

"Then I'm pretty sure you'd be a spelunker," Lacy said, her eyes twinkling.

Hannah chuckled. "Fair enough."

"Ready?"

"Sure thing." Hannah hauled the books to the circulation desk, where Evangeline checked them out, and then they stepped outside. There was a slight chill in the air, which felt delightful after the heated air of the library.

"Where to next?" Lacy asked.

"The pawn shop."

"You really know how to hit the highlights."

"Maybe we'll get lucky and find it still exists."

"We can only hope." Lacy's tone was dry.

"There's still a dirty chicken coop waiting for you, if you'd rather do that."

Lacy grinned. "Lead the way."

P—

I know I owed you the cash yesterday. I'm working on it, and I'll get it.

I just need a little more time.

It's coming.

—C

Chapter Six

Hannah checked the address at the bottom of the pawn shop receipt. When she was growing up, this block was considered a seedy part of town, with a few bars and pawn shops and a lot of empty storefronts. That was no longer the case, and the street was lined with shops and lively businesses. They passed a paper goods store, a copy shop, an accountant's office, and an artisanal ice cream shop, which advertised flavors like Salted Honeycomb and Praline Butter Cake. Someone had planted young trees in the pits along the sidewalk. They were small but bursting with fiery orange leaves. In a few years, they would be beautiful.

"This is so different from what this part of town used to be," Hannah said as she parked.

"People have been putting a lot of time and care into the area," Lacy said. "At first artsy people moved in because they could afford to live here and make art, and then all this happened." She gestured around.

"I'm doubting there's still a pawn shop along this strip."

"Yeah, it doesn't seem likely," Lacy said.

They counted down the numbers above the doors and finally found the right building, which now housed a florist shop called Blackberry Blooms on the ground floor. Beautiful ferns and rubber plants graced the large plate-glass windows, and bouquets stood in buckets inside the shop.

"Should we go in?" Lacy asked.

"I guess we might as well see if they can tell us anything about what this used to be," Hannah said, though she was dubious. She pushed open the door, and the sweet scent of roses, lilacs, and lavender hit her.

"It smells heavenly in here," Lacy said, closing the door behind her. The shop was small, with white beadboard walls and wide-plank wooden floors that creaked under their steps.

"Thank you. It does make for a nice space to work," said the woman behind the counter. She was young and had platinum-blond hair with several inches of dark roots showing, big glasses, and tattoos all along her bare arms. Hannah recognized her as the younger sister of a classmate she'd had named Nicki Bronson. She forgot what this younger sister's name was though. Noelle? Holly? She thought it was something Christmassy.

"Winter," Lacy said with a smile. "It's so good to see you. I didn't know this was your place."

Winter. Well, she'd been close.

"Hi, Lacy. I just opened it this summer," Winter said. "It's going well so far."

"Do you remember Hannah Prentiss? She was the same year as Nicki and me." Lacy gestured to Hannah.

"Hey." Winter smiled at her. "It's good to see you. I'd heard you were back in town. That new restaurant is yours, right?"

"That's right," Hannah said.

"I've been meaning to try it," Winter said.

"I'd love to see you there. And this place is beautiful," Hannah said. "How's Nicki doing?"

"Amazing. She lives in Atlanta and just had her second baby." Winter whipped out her phone and showed them photos.

"Gorgeous," Lacy said.

"And what have you been up to?" Hannah asked.

"Well, I went to college and got a degree in botany before moving home. I worked at a landscaping company for a few years, saving up and building experience, before I opened this shop. It's a dream come true." She straightened a floral arrangement that sat on the counter. "So, what brings you in here today?"

"We were actually hoping to learn more about a business that used to be in this space years ago," Hannah said. Winter's face fell, and she quickly added, "But now that I'm here, I can't leave without some flowers. Those peonies are gorgeous. You normally don't see them this time of year." She pulled a bunch of delicate pale-pink flowers from a round metal bin. A few drops of water splashed to the floor.

"They're grown in a greenhouse not far from here," Winter said, her face brightening again. "My old professor owns it."

"It's such a treat to see them," Hannah said. "I can't resist."

Winter took the flowers from her, wrapped them in brown paper, and tied it off with brown twine. As she rang up the purchase, she said, "I'm not sure how much I can tell you about what was here before this shop. The space was empty for about six months before I leased it. It was a clothing shop for older women a few years before that, so I wasn't super familiar with it."

"It was a pawn shop back in 1960," Hannah said.

"Huh." Winter shrugged. "That was well before my time."

"So you've never spoken to anyone associated with the pawn shop?" Hannah asked.

"Nope." Winter handed her the bouquet. "You could ask Karen DiSalvo. She owns the building, but she just bought it a few years ago, so she probably wouldn't be able to tell you about what it was like in the sixties."

Hannah didn't know what she'd hoped for, but she could tell they weren't going find it with Winter. She stored the wrapped bouquet into her tote bag and was extra careful as she slipped the straps over her shoulder to avoid crushing it.

"Thank you so much," she said. "We appreciate it. And good luck with the shop. It's really beautiful."

"Thank you. I'll swing by your restaurant the next time I get a chance." Winter waved as they walked out the door.

"Well, that wasn't especially useful, but at least you got some pretty flowers out of it," Lacy said. "Are you going to contact Karen?"

"I haven't decided yet. I don't know how likely it is that I'll find anything useful from this line of inquiry, to be honest," Hannah said. "I mean, I guess I was hoping to find whoever was there when Chuck went to pawn his things, but that seems pretty unlikely."

"It *was* more than sixty years ago," Lacy agreed. "Even if we could find that person, what would they be able to tell us? Do you think Chuck would have told them what he was planning while he sold his valuables for cash?"

"No, probably not," Hannah said with a sigh. "Though if he had, it certainly would make things easier."

"If he had and you could find that person now, it would be amazing. Not to mention a small miracle," Lacy said.

"I guess I'll move the pawn shop lead to the back burner," Hannah said.

"So what's on the front burner?"

"I say we should go and talk to Neil," Hannah said. "Though I could use some coffee first."

"You won't get any argument from me," Lacy said. "Besides, it's on the way."

Lacy drove to Main Street and parked in front of Jump Start Coffee. Hannah left the books and flowers in the pickup, and they walked inside. The high ceilings and warm wooden floors made the space feel open and inviting, and most of the tables were occupied by people chatting in small groups or pecking away at laptops. Zane Forrest, who owned the shop—and was the brother of Hannah's head chef, Jacob—was behind the register taking orders.

"Hi, Zane," Hannah said as she stepped up to the counter. "Just a latte for me, please."

"Sure thing. For here or to go?" Zane had several days' worth of scruff and thick-framed glasses, and he wore jeans and a black T-shirt. He had a much more laid-back appearance than his brother, but Hannah knew him well enough to know that his work ethic was every bit as strong as Jacob's.

"To go, please."

"Coming right up."

While they waited, Hannah scanned the small shop. She recognized several people from church and regulars at the restaurant, and there was Dylan hunched over a thick book and a laptop at a back table.

Hannah decided it would be weird not to say hello, so after she got her coffee, she went over to his table. "Hi, Dylan."

Dylan immediately put his arms over the open book on the table in front of him. "Hey, Hannah. How are you?" His voice was too high, and his cheerful greeting sounded forced.

"I'm okay. Doing some work on your day off?" What work could he possibly have to do though? He wasn't in school as far as she knew.

"Totally." He grinned. "This is a good place to do it. Gets me out of the house."

"And the coffee is good." Hannah held up her cup, hoping to make the encounter less awkward. "Well, enjoy."

"You too." Dylan didn't move his arms, and Hannah and Lacy walked out of the shop. As they started along Main Street, Hannah could see through the window that Dylan was staring down at his book once again.

"That was weird," Hannah said.

"What?"

"Dylan's in there studying something, but he obviously didn't want me to see what it is."

"What's weird about not wanting your boss to know your personal business?" Lacy took a sip from her drink, and Hannah could smell the pumpkin-spice scent wafting out of her cup. "It doesn't seem strange to me."

"When you say it like that, it doesn't sound so odd, but something about it was awkward. It was almost like he was embarrassed to be caught working on something."

"You're making it sound like he's up to something nefarious," Lacy said. "But he wouldn't be doing anything wrong in a public coffee shop. He probably just didn't want to have an awkward conversation with his boss. And it's not really any of your business what he was doing on his day off anyway, is it?"

Lacy was right. It wasn't any of her business, and there was probably nothing strange about the interaction. But her curiosity still lingered. Today's encounter, coupled with the strange way he'd been acting on Saturday night, made her wonder what was up.

Well, as Lacy said, it wasn't her place to speculate about what was going on. And they were almost at the bookstore anyway.

The big front window of the shop was set with a display of various historical fiction titles, and Hannah loved seeing the old-fashioned clothing and the different settings from around the world on the book covers. LEGEND & KEY BOOKSTORE was written on the plate glass in gold lettering. Anyone who could resist such a display was clearly not a bookworm at heart.

Lacy walked into the bookstore first, and Hannah followed a step behind her. The little bell over the door rang cheerily as they opened and closed it behind them. Tables at the front of the shop displayed bestselling and new books, and beyond that were rows of wooden shelves stocked with new and used books on every subject. A cozy children's area was at the back, and a small seating area with two armchairs took up the open space next to the antique fireplace.

As they walked inside, Hannah's eye caught on the bright cover of a new cozy mystery in a series she loved on one of the front tables. She set her coffee on the table and picked up the book.

"Welcome," Neil called from somewhere in one of the aisles. A moment later, he emerged, and his face broke out into a wide smile when he saw who it was. "Hello. What brings you two in here this morning? I'm assuming it was to see the handsome bookshop owner?"

Lacy laughed and leaned in to give him a kiss. "It was, actually."

"Though I may be tempted by this," Hannah said, turning the book over in her hands. Sure, she already had several books from the library in Lacy's car, but she'd never been able to resist the lure of a good book, and this series was one of her favorites, featuring an American veterinarian from Connecticut who moved to Yorkshire to take over her late grandfather's practice.

"That's a really good one," Neil said, nodding at Hannah. "The best in the series, in my opinion."

As much as she loved her own job, she sometimes envied people who got to read and call it work like Neil did. "Sold."

"Easiest sale of the day," Neil said with a laugh. "Now, what can I help you with?"

"We wanted to show you a map," Lacy said. "An old one."

"Now you're just flirting with me. I'm a married man, you know." Neil waved them over to the counter.

Hannah set her coffee and the book on the counter and her bag on the floor. Neil moved aside a display of bookmarks to make space for her to spread the map out. The side that showed Kentucky was face up.

"This is a fun one," Neil said. "Before the interstate came through."

"It's from 1958, according to the copyright," Lacy said.

"I was going to guess somewhere in that era," Neil said. He lifted the map to glance at the back, nodding when he saw that it showed the state of Tennessee. "So what are we looking for?" He laid the map down again.

"We're not exactly sure," Lacy admitted.

"It belonged to my great-uncle," Hannah said. "Before he disappeared."

"Ah. This is one of the things from the cave?"

Hannah wasn't surprised Lacy had told him about the discovery on their property.

"That's right," Hannah said. "And as you can see, there are circles around three cities. We were hoping you'd be able to help us make sense of which one he went to."

"I'm a map lover, not a mind reader," Neil said. "But let me take a look." He leaned over the map and studied the pencil-drawn circles around Lexington and Louisville and then flipped it over and studied the one around Nashville.

"I don't know," he finally said. "I can tell you that some of the towns on this map have grown and some have shrunk since it was published, and that the route of the interstate had a lot to do with that, but I can't tell you where your great-uncle went based on this. I'm sorry."

"That's okay," Hannah said. "I guess I was asking for a miracle."

"Miracles do happen," Neil said. "But in this case, I'm afraid I don't know what to tell you."

"No problem." Hannah started folding the map.

"But I do have a map that shows the cave system under this area, or what we know of it anyway, if you want to see that." Neil cocked his head.

Hannah returned the map to the plastic storage bag and replaced it in her tote bag. "Really? That would be great."

"Come on." He gestured for them to follow him to the rear of the store. Hannah expected him to lead them to the bin of antique maps there, but instead he walked over to a section of guidebooks and travel guides. He selected one from the shelf, and Hannah saw that it was a guidebook called *Caving in Barren County.*

"That's a niche title if I ever saw one," Lacy said.

"We don't sell many copies of it, but every once in a while it's exactly what someone is looking for," Neil said. He opened the book and thumbed through it then stopped on a page with a section entitled "McLeod Cave." He angled the book so Hannah and Lacy could see it. "Here we go."

Hannah leaned in and saw two line drawings on the page. It took a moment for her to make sense of them, but then she saw that the first one showed the cave from above, with each underground chamber and corridor marked. The second drawing showed it from the side, with the entrance marked at the top and the chambers cascading down as they went deeper underground. Looking at them both, it was clear how complex the cave was, with its many caverns connected by narrow crawl spaces branching off in every direction, as well as how deep it went.

There were symbols in many places on the map, and a key at the bottom indicated that they marked things like ceiling height, water in the cavern, slopes, and something called breakdown. A quick online search on her phone told her that referred to the debris left when part of a cave collapsed. There were also several places where the corridors ended and were marked as possible or certain connections to other caves. There were sections of the cave labeled *Jim's Tight Squeeze, Belly Crawl*, and *Confusion Tubes.* Hannah was even more convinced that people who willingly went down into caves like this were nuts.

"The cavern where Chuck's things were discovered is here," Neil said, pointing to a chamber about halfway down the second map. It was labeled *The Boneyard.* She'd read that in one of the articles, but it still sounded creepy. "You can see that the chamber used to be connected to the tunnel, but here they've marked it as separate." He ran his finger over the map, tapping the relevant spots. "These little diamond shapes here are for breakdown, and that shows this area is cut off because of rockfall."

Studying the map, Hannah could follow what he was saying. "So once that section collapsed, this chamber was entirely cut off from the rest of the cave."

"It was believed to be," Neil said. "Until Saturday, when your cousin and Colt discovered another entrance by descending into it."

There was nothing marking the way they'd gone in, but that made sense if it hadn't been discovered before the two guys came across it. It was crazy to think that they had found something no one else had ever discovered before. She wondered if they would get to name it. *Ryder's Scary Descent.* Or maybe *Colt's Death Wish.*

"That entrance would have to be here," Hannah said, pointing to the top of the closed-off cavern. "Which means they would have descended from this area." She indicated the section of cavern above it, where there was another small cavern marked as *Unexplored.*

"This map will need to be updated," Neil said. "They're always a work in progress, as new parts of the caverns are explored and when weather or human activity moves the rock and closes off portions."

Hannah appreciated the map, as it helped her visualize how the cave branched out underground from the entrance, but she couldn't see anything that might explain how Chuck's things ended up there.

"If you're interested in caving, this is a great guide to the area," Neil said, the smile on his face making it clear he was joking.

"No thank you," Hannah said. "I'll just take the mystery, if it's all the same to you. But is it okay if I take a picture of this page?"

"Sure." Neil let her take the photo then put the book back on the shelf. Hannah and Lacy followed him to the front of the store, where he rang up the mystery novel.

When she and Lacy stepped out of the store, Lacy asked, "What now?"

"I don't know," Hannah said. "I'm not sure we learned much of anything today."

"That's not true. We know that Chuck didn't go to Lexington or Louisville. At least not using his real name."

"You're right, but that doesn't exactly help us much." Hannah sighed. "I wish the police were working on this. They have so many more resources than we do."

"It *is* a small force," Lacy reminded her. "I'm sure they've got other priorities."

"There's hardly any crime in Blackberry Valley," Hannah said. "How busy could they be?"

"The police do plenty of other things besides solve crimes," Lacy said. She slid her arm through Hannah's. "And by the way, what are the resources they have that you don't?"

"Badges, for one," Hannah said.

"What good is a badge for a case that's over half a century old?"

"They can get people to talk," Hannah said.

"Like who? Anyone relevant is someone you're already reaching out to," Lacy said.

Hannah didn't want to admit it, but the more she thought about it, the more she realized Lacy was right.

"Okay, but what about the old police file?" Hannah said. "They can see all the evidence that was collected back then."

"You can get that too, can't you?" Lacy said. "Anyone can request records from the state, right?"

"You can stop having all the answers whenever you want," Hannah informed her friend.

"But if I did that, we'd be totally stuck," Lacy replied.

Hannah elbowed her. "I guess we could go to the station and see if they can share the file with us."

"It would be better than pouting," Lacy said.

They'd been friends long enough that Lacy could say things like that. "Fine," Hannah said. "Let's go."

Chapter Seven

When they walked into the police station, Vanessa Lodge looked up from her computer and greeted them. She sat at the front of the large open room, and Hannah could see Deputy Jacky Holt talking on the phone at her desk behind Vanessa.

"Hello," Vanessa said, smiling. No matter how busy her job was, she was always cheerful. "How can I help you ladies this morning?"

"We were hoping to see an old police file," Hannah said. "From back in the sixties."

"Let me guess. You want the one about the guy who was trapped in that cave? Or, well, actually wasn't?"

"Good guess," Hannah said.

"It wasn't exactly hard, given that you two were there when his things were discovered, and that Ryder said you were hoping the department would be able to look into it, since the man was your great-uncle."

"Ryder told me there was no such luck," Hannah said.

"Apparently not," Vanessa said. "I know the sheriff checked the file, but I think he may be done with it. In any case, if you want to request it, you need to fill this out." She pulled a form out of her drawer and slid it across the desk.

Hannah took a pen from the cup on the desk and started to fill out the page. It asked for the names of the people involved, relevant dates, and lots of other information that seemed extraneous since Vanessa knew exactly which file she was asking about. But she filled it out as best she could.

"I'll check on this and let you know what I find out," Vanessa said, taking the form from her.

Hannah thanked her, and she and Lacy left the station.

"Now what?" Hannah said as they walked to Lacy's truck.

"Honestly, I probably need to get back to the farm," Lacy said. "Cleaning the henhouses can't be avoided forever."

Hannah sighed. She should probably get around to her list of tasks she'd planned to accomplish sometime that day.

"You're coming over for puzzle night tonight, right?" Lacy asked.

"I wouldn't miss it." Lacy's monthly puzzle nights were always a fun time.

Lacy dropped her off in front of the Hot Spot, and Hannah carried her flowers and the books she'd gathered up the stairs to her apartment and set them on her kitchen table. She eyed the books from the library. Those would be interesting to flip through, but she itched to dive into the mystery. That would be a nice reward when she finished all the tasks on her list for the day. For now, she would head downstairs to the restaurant to start processing invoices.

She trotted down the stairs and into the restaurant. As much as she loved the energy and excitement of the restaurant when it was full, she also loved the peacefulness when it was empty and quiet like this. She kept the lights in the dining room off as she made her way to the office in the back and then sat at the computer and turned it on.

The first thing she did was check her email, and she was pleased to see that she had a letter from her father's cousin Roger.

Hannah,

It's great to hear from you. I remember you fondly as the little girl in braids who made the best grilled cheese sandwich I've ever eaten, still to this day. I suppose you're not a little girl in braids any longer. Aunt Elsa told me that you own a restaurant now, and I can't wait to try it out.

I was glad to get your email. My father's things being found in the cave is news to me for sure, and I would very much like to know more about it.

I work from home most days. I looked up the Hot Spot online and saw your business hours. Since it's open only for dinner, I was thinking that if you were free one morning this week, I could take a break from my work if you could come out this way. I'd love to see you. Just let me know when.

Best,

Roger

Hannah checked her calendar and saw that any morning this week should be okay. But she didn't necessarily want to go see Roger alone. She called her dad.

"Hey, Hannah. How's it going?" Dad asked when he picked up.

"Hi, Dad. I'm good. I heard back from Roger, and he's invited me to come out to see him to talk about Chuck. Do you have time to go with me some morning this week?" Her father was a retired electrician, but he was involved in plenty of activities and men's groups, and she didn't know his schedule.

"Sure I do. When do you want to go?"

Hannah didn't want to wait. "How about tomorrow?"

"That sounds good to me."

"Great. I'll make sure that works for Roger and let you know."

"I'm looking forward to it."

Hannah sent an email to Roger asking whether Tuesday worked, and then she turned to her invoices and payroll. Many people didn't realize how much paperwork was involved in owning a restaurant. It wasn't her favorite part of the job, but it had to be done.

A few hours later, she checked her email before she went back upstairs, and found that Roger had confirmed that he was free for a visit tomorrow morning. Hannah let her dad know and then went upstairs to her apartment to get ready to go to Lacy's.

Hannah hummed while she prepared the pumpkin ravioli she'd promised to bring to puzzle night. While she waited for the water to boil, she started looking through the books she'd checked out from the library.

First, she paged through the guidebook to caves in Kentucky. It was far less detailed than the one she'd seen in Neil's shop, but it talked about caves all over the state, instead of just Barren County. She found a few pages of general information about each of the caves, and it seemed to focus on the more well-known ones, such as Diamond Caverns, Onyx Cave, Hidden River Cave—where visitors could ride a boat through the underground river—and, of course, Mammoth Cave National Park. The largest known cave system in the world, Mammoth

Cave was over four hundred miles long and filled with interesting caverns. Hannah concluded that the book was more a guide for tourists than for serious cavers. As interesting as it was, it didn't include any entries for McLeod Cave, so she didn't think it would be of much use.

She set that book aside and paged through the one about the geology of how the underground caverns formed, but her eyes quickly glazed over.

> *Caves in this region are primarily made of limestone, sandstone, and shale, formed by groundwater seeping between layers of limestone, dissolving minerals and creating small channels, which were enlarged over time...*

Hannah was sure the information was all interesting and important, but it didn't really help with her current question, so she set that book aside also. She flipped through the caver's memoir, but she would need to come back to that one, as she wasn't sure how relevant it would be.

She turned to the final book in her stack, a reference book of caving terminology and pictures of cave formations. There were photos of those that were more commonly known, such as stalactites and stalagmites—long, skinny rock formations on the ceiling and floor of caverns, created by minerals deposited from water dripping within the cave—as well as less commonly known formations. Flowstone resembled frozen waterfalls. Cave popcorn was formed when water seeped through pores in limestone to create little knobs of calcite. Dripping water could crystalize into hollow tubes of rock called soda straws. There was drapery that looked like curtains, and cave bacon that looked exactly as Hannah thought it would from the name.

Admiring the photos, Hannah could almost see the appeal of navigating these underground caverns. Almost. It was amazing to see so many beautiful creations formed underground.

The book also defined caving terms. Hannah wasn't surprised to find that caving, like most hobbies, seemed to have its own language, and she read through the list, trying to get a feel for the sport. There was one term she'd seen a few times in the other books but hadn't understood: *karst*. That meant a limestone-rich landscape, often home to caves, sinks, and springs. Apparently, the area around Blackberry Valley was a karst.

She also read about pits, which were shafts that required specialized equipment to descend into. A show cave was one that had been modified so the public could visit. Eardippers were passages where cavers had to pass through a low spot filled with water. She shuddered when she found the term *boneyard*, even when the book explained that it was merely a sheet of limestone that had eroded to leave bone-like shapes behind. She also found the term *boulder choke*, which was a mass of rubble or rocks that blocked a passage. She supposed it was a boulder choke that had sealed off the passage where Chuck's things were found.

Which was all very interesting, but didn't get her any closer to what had happened to Chuck. She closed the book and got up to get ready to head to Lacy's. The day had been an exercise in frustration. Nothing she'd done had gotten her any closer to finding out what had happened to Chuck. Hopefully she'd find some answers when she talked to Roger tomorrow.

Lucky—

I'm told you know a guy who does papers.

Good ones, that pass for real.

Can you put me in touch with him?

—C

Chapter Eight

Hannah picked her dad up just after nine on Tuesday morning. As he climbed into the car, she held out a cup of coffee and a doughnut she'd picked up from Sweet Caroline's on the way over.

"You're too good to me," he said as he buckled himself in. Then he accepted the doughnut and took a bite. "Boston cream. My favorite."

"Every kind of doughnut is your favorite, as long as you actually get to eat it," Hannah teased.

"Too true," he agreed, smiling.

"It's a small way to say thanks for coming with me," Hannah said. Plus, it gave her an excuse to have one of their maple bars, which were to die for.

"I'm excited to see Roger. It's been too long. I don't think I've seen him since your mother's funeral."

"I vaguely remember saying hello to him there, but honestly the whole thing was kind of a blur."

"I understand that," Dad said. "Anyway, Roger's a cool guy. He works at the Corvette Museum."

"That's what makes him cool?" The Corvette Museum in Bowling Green was exactly what it sounded like—a museum that showcased the history of the famed sports car. It was not far from the factory that manufactured the cars.

"Of course that's not what makes him cool. But you have to admit, it's a cool job."

"I guess so." She shrugged. "Corvettes aren't very practical cars." Dad had always driven pickup trucks that he could use to haul around equipment for his job.

"They're not supposed to be practical. They're fast, and they look good. What more do you need?"

Hannah laughed. "What can you tell me about Roger besides the fact he has a cool job?" she asked as she merged onto the highway.

"Let's see." Dad took another bite of his doughnut and sat back in his seat. After a moment he said, "When he would come to visit your uncle Gordon and me when we were kids, he always wanted to play baseball. That kid was obsessed. He had a huge baseball card collection. And he loved spaghetti. That was his favorite meal."

"Okay. Anything more relevant to this mystery?"

"Picky, picky. Let's see. I don't remember Chuck, obviously. I was only a tiny baby when he disappeared. But Aunt Minnie remarried, and Uncle Don was the best. He had a big laugh, he liked to fish, and he always carried around hard candy."

"He raised Roger?"

"Roger was Uncle Don's son, in every way except biology, so every way that really mattered, to my way of thinking. He adopted Roger and was as good a father as my own."

"I'm glad of that." Hannah thought for a minute. "Roger's married, right?"

"He was for many years. His wife died about ten years ago."

That explained why she didn't remember Roger's wife being at Mom's funeral with him. "He has kids, right?"

"Two boys, Stephen and Eric. Stephen works on space shuttles in Houston. Talk about a cool job. And Eric lives nearby with his wife and son."

They talked more about Dad's memories of Roger as a kid while they drove, and soon they reached a subdivision in Bowling Green with large houses set on small plots of land. They found his house—brick, two-story, lots of gables and black ironwork—easily enough. Hannah picked up the bag of things that had been found in the cave and carried it to the door, where her dad rang the doorbell. A man with white hair and glasses answered the door. He looked pretty much the same as she remembered, just a bit older.

"Gabriel. Hannah. So good to see you." Roger ushered them inside and hugged both of them. "Thank you for coming out here."

"Thank you for meeting with us," Hannah said. The entryway had a double-height vaulted ceiling and a staircase that twisted as it rose. A living room was to one side, and a dining room to the other. She could see a kitchen with high-end appliances and granite counters from where she stood.

"Of course. I'm obviously very interested to hear more about what you all found in that cave. If he didn't die in there, that changes everything, doesn't it?" He led them into the living room. "I mean, my whole life…" He trailed off then shook himself. "Please, take a seat. Go ahead and set that on the coffee table," he said, indicating the bag. "Can I get you anything? Coffee? Water?"

"No thank you," Hannah said. Her father echoed her, and they sat down on a blue-and-white striped couch. The room had a nautical theme, with a brass admiral's mirror over the mantel, a replica of a sailing ship on a side table, and a wooden ship's steering wheel and framed paintings of sailboats on the walls. It seemed like an odd choice for southern Kentucky, but it was an elegant room.

Roger took a seat in a matching wingback. "So, are those his things?"

"That's right." Hannah took out her cell phone and pulled up the photos taken inside the cave. "As you can see, they were discovered in a neat pile in the sealed-off cavern, as if they were placed there intentionally."

Roger studied the screen, and then he began to take the items out of the bag, one at a time. He examined the map, apparently noting the cities Chuck had circled, and the bus receipt.

"This bus station closed years ago," Roger said, holding up the receipt. "It's a fast-food restaurant now."

"What a shame." Though she knew no one who worked at the station in 1960 would still be there, Hannah had half-hoped they might be able to swing by there while they were in town.

Next Roger picked up the pawn shop bill of sale, then the pants and shirt, and then he set them down and picked up the wallet. He slid the driver's license out of the pocket. "That's his, no doubt," Roger said. "And you're right, the items he left behind and the way they were all placed sure make it seem like it wasn't an accident. Like he put them there on purpose and just...left."

There was deep sorrow in his voice. Hannah couldn't imagine what he must be feeling, trying to come to terms with the fact that his father hadn't truly died but willingly walked away from him.

"I'm glad Mom never found out about this," Roger said. "She would not have taken it well."

"I don't imagine there are too many people who would," Dad said.

"What did your mom tell you about your father's death?" Hannah asked.

"She didn't talk about it much," Roger said. "And when she did, she seemed to see it as a blessing, honestly. She always told me that he'd gone and gotten himself killed and left gambling debts she got stuck paying. It wasn't very flattering, the way she talked about him."

"It sounded like things were hard for them," Dad said.

"Yes, I think they must have been. Luckily, she ended up finding Don. That's the man I've always called my father. By all accounts, he was everything Chuck wasn't. He was stable and kind and the best kind of father I can imagine."

"I'm so glad," Hannah said.

"Despite everything else she said about him, Mom always made a point of telling me that Chuck loved me," Roger said. "She never wanted me to doubt that, which I appreciate. She used to say that the only thing he loved more than gambling was me. Which I guess is flattering, in a way."

"I'm sure she wouldn't have said it if it wasn't true," Dad said.

Roger shrugged. "Anyway, after you got in touch, Hannah, I went down to the basement and found this." He indicated a shoebox with the word CHUCK written in thick marker. "It's a few things Mom held on to from him. I thought you might like to see it, in case there's anything in here that might tell us more about what happened."

Hannah leaned forward and took the lid off the box, which was covered in a fine layer of dust. Inside, she found a handful of photographs, as well as a couple of letters, a bracelet made of a leather cord, and a guitar pick.

"Is this him?" Hannah picked up a photograph of a man in jeans and a black T-shirt holding the lead of a beautiful roan horse. He was blond, with rugged good looks, and he was tan and fit, with an air of confidence about him.

"That's him, back when he cared for the horses on Bluegrass Hollow Farm," Roger said.

"He was quite handsome, wasn't he?" Hannah said.

"'Too pretty for his own good' is how Mom always described him. She said she should have seen through him, but she was taken in by his good looks." Roger shook his head. "She said he managed to get away with way more than he should have, and that was part of why he never grew up enough to take care of a wife and child."

There were clearly some tough feelings there, and Hannah couldn't fault him or his mother for that. She flipped to the next photo in the bunch, which was a shot of Chuck in a suit and Minnie in a pale lavender dress, holding a bunch of wildflowers. There was a slight thickening at her waist.

"That was their wedding day," Chuck said. "They went down to city hall."

"They look happy," Hannah said, and they did, though there was also some reserve in Minnie's smile. As if she was unsure, even then.

"I don't know whether they would have gotten married if not for me," Roger said. "That wasn't a nice feeling. But Mom always insisted she wouldn't change a thing. I suppose she had to say that, but she made sure I felt she meant it."

"I'm sure she did." Hannah handed the first two photos to her dad and looked at the next, which showed Chuck in a hat with a headlamp on it, holding a rope. He stood in front of a cave entrance.

"I don't know what cave that is or who took the photo," Roger said. "Frankly, I hate caves, and you couldn't get me near one, so I can't tell you anything more than that."

"That makes sense, given your history." Hannah passed the photograph to her dad and turned her attention to the last one, which showed four men. Hannah quickly picked out Chuck, standing on the left side, holding a fiddle. The man to his right had a guitar, and there was also a bass player and a man playing a banjo.

"He was a musician." Hannah had almost forgotten. That was how Minnie first met him, at one of his shows.

"He was into bluegrass, mostly, from what I'm told," Roger said. "These were some guys he played with back in the day, I guess."

"Do you know who the other men are?" Dad asked.

Roger shook his head. "Not a clue, I'm afraid."

Hannah flipped the photograph over and saw someone had written their names on the back. *Chuck Lynch, George Grey, Harold Summers, Arturo Vargas, 1957.* Hannah wondered about the other men. Did any of them know anything about what had happened to Chuck?

Hannah used her phone to take a picture of each of the photos and also the back of the shot of the musicians so she could remember all their names. She examined the bracelet and the guitar pick, searching for any sort of clue that would tell her more about what had happened to Chuck.

"There's not a lot here, I know." Roger was quiet for a moment then added, "Some of Mom's things are in the basement, including a few of her diaries. I don't know if they would tell us more. I tried looking at one when she passed, but I haven't read through them. It was too hard at the time. But I couldn't bring myself to get rid of them either."

"I felt the same way about my wife's journals," Hannah's dad said.

Hannah had wondered more than once what had happened to her mom's journals, but had never asked. She'd have to talk to Dad about it and see if he was okay with her going through them. It would help her feel connected to Mom again.

"Please don't feel obligated to share your mother's diaries if you're not comfortable with it," Hannah said to Roger.

"Normally I wouldn't be, but I do want to know what happened to my biological father, and those diaries might provide some clue." Roger stood. "In any case, I think it's worth finding out." He strode from the room.

There was a bookcase against the far wall, and in addition to hardback volumes wedged in between brass anchor bookends, there was a cluster of framed photographs. Hannah pushed herself up and walked over to see them better. There was one of Roger and likely his two grown sons on a windswept beach. There was one of a smiling baby—no doubt Roger's grandson.

Hannah spotted a family photo taken in the eighties, guessing by the coloring on the print and the fashions and feathered hair. Roger and a woman who must be his late wife stood with their young sons in front of a sign that read *Fisherman's Wharf*. A family trip to San Francisco, then. There were a couple of Eric and Stephen when they were children, and a black-and-white photo that might have been Roger when he was a toddler. There was a wedding picture of one of the sons, likely Eric.

"Here's what I found," Roger said, carrying half a dozen journals of different sizes and colors into the room. He set the stack on the coffee table and lifted one bound in black leather. "This one is from the era when Chuck disappeared. I don't know if I can bring myself to…" His voice trailed off, and he grimaced at the book.

"I'll look it over, if that's all right with you," Hannah volunteered.

"Thank you." Roger settled back into his chair, relief clear on his face. "When I was downstairs, I thought about something. An incident that seemed strange at the time, although I didn't think too much about it. But now that I know about my father, I can't help but wonder."

"What happened?" Hannah asked as she sat down again.

Roger hesitated before answering, as if he was gathering his thoughts. "It was probably fifteen years ago. I was watching the baseball game in the living room when a man came to the door and asked to borrow a phone. He was an older guy. Not really old, you understand, but older than me. He said his car broke down, his cell phone was dead, and he needed to call someone. I was happy to help, of course, but it struck me as odd that he'd come here. It's not like we're out in the country and ours is the only house around. There are a dozen houses on this block, and we're in the middle."

"And a subdivision isn't the kind of place where you just wind up with car trouble and no one to ask for help," Dad said. "Usually, you're there because you live there or you're visiting someone who does."

"Exactly." Roger nodded. "So it seemed odd. I let him use my phone, of course. But he behaved strangely."

"How so?"

"Once I handed him the phone, he wasn't especially interested in using it," Roger said. "He asked a lot of questions about me. What

I did, whether I liked the area, if I had any kids, how they were doing in school—that kind of thing. It was kind of creepy. I was home alone, which I was thankful for at the time. He told me he was a bluegrass musician on his way to a gig in Nashville."

"And his car broke down here? In this subdivision?" Hannah asked. Bowling Green was on a major highway that led to Nashville, so that wasn't totally implausible, but it didn't seem likely that his car trouble led him to this house by accident.

"And it didn't stop there," Roger said. "He took the phone into the dining room to make the call. Then he brought it back and left. I saw him get into a car and drive off."

"What about his car trouble?" Dad asked.

"Fixed, I guess." Roger shrugged. "And when I checked my phone later, I saw that he hadn't actually called anybody."

"Did you inform the police?" Dad asked. "I would have."

"No, but we did install a security system after that," Roger said. "But the reason I didn't was—well, I'd never met the guy before, and the whole thing was odd, but somehow he seemed kind of familiar to me at the time."

Hannah felt goose bumps rise on her arms. If this was going where she thought it was…

"Of course, I never imagined—I mean, Dad had supposedly been dead for decades by that point," Roger said. "And I was so young when he died that I didn't have any memories of him."

"You think it was him?" Dad asked.

"On his way out, he introduced himself." Roger clasped his hands together. "He said his name was Charles."

Ricky, running a little late. I had to make a stop in Bowling Green.

How late, Chuck? The opening band is about to go on.

I'll be there before we go on. Sorry. It was important.

I'd better not find out you "had" to stop to see some chick.

Nothing like that. Like I said, it was important. I'll be there soon.

Chapter Nine

Hannah was still processing the revelation that Chuck had stopped in and met his grown son without revealing who he was when they got on the road to drive back to Blackberry Valley.

"How can we know if it was really Chuck?" she asked. "It's pure conjecture at this point."

"Conjecture, plus the fact that he told him his name was Charles," Dad said.

"There are many Charleses in the world," Hannah said. "Still, it would be quite a coincidence if it wasn't him."

"Especially given everything else Roger said about the man," Dad agreed. "That he was older, that he asked all about Roger and his family, that he didn't end up needing the phone, that Roger thought he seemed familiar."

"Okay, so let's assume it was Chuck." Hannah pulled onto the highway. "What do we know about him?"

"We know he knew where Roger lived," Dad said. "He knew where to find him."

Hannah nodded. "And we can assume this means Chuck wanted to meet him. But he didn't want to reveal who he was."

"How could he? They all thought he was dead. And he wanted them to think that."

"He vanished and started a new life somewhere else."

"If Roger's visitor was indeed Chuck, we know his father was alive fifteen years ago," Dad said.

"Right," Hannah said. "We know that he was traveling to a gig in Nashville, if he was telling the truth."

"Let's assume he was, since he told Roger his real name."

"Right. So, if he was traveling *to* Nashville, it means he didn't live *in* Nashville. So that's one city we can cross off the list."

"And we know he's a bluegrass musician. Or said he was."

"So we need to look into bluegrass musicians. How many could there be?"

"In Kentucky?" Dad laughed. "A lot."

"It's a place to start," Hannah said. "And we have Minnie's diaries. We can read through those and see if there's anything that will tell us more about Chuck's disappearance. We also have the names of the guys Chuck was in that band with. I can try to see if any of them are still around, and if they know anything."

It wasn't a lot to go on, but it was more than they'd had that morning. They talked about the visit the whole way back to Blackberry Valley. Hannah dropped Dad off at the house he shared with Uncle Gabriel then unloaded the diaries at her apartment. She needed to get down to the restaurant, but she couldn't stop thinking about Roger as she helped Jacob chop apples for the dessert special. Jacob usually did his own prep, but repetitive tasks like this allowed Hannah space to think. So she chopped apples and mixed pie dough while Jacob worked on getting the burger patties shaped and the bacon cooked.

If they were right, Chuck was alive fifteen years ago. But a lot could happen in fifteen years, and Chuck would be in his eighties now if he was still around.

Assuming he hadn't gone to Nashville, she could narrow in on Lexington and Louisville as his more likely destinations. Of course, just because he had gone to any city sixty years ago didn't mean he was there now. How hard could it be to find bluegrass musicians in those places, even from fifteen years ago? But where would she even start to look them up?

Before she knew it, the rest of the staff had arrived and everything was ready for opening. Hannah's sister-in-law, Allison, was the first person to walk inside for dinner.

"Good evening," Elaine greeted her.

"Hi, Elaine. Hi, Hannah," Allison said, letting the door fall closed behind her. "It smells so good in here." Her long auburn hair hung loose, and she wore a cute top with jeans and ballet flats.

"Just one?" Hannah asked. Perhaps the busy wife and mother of three was taking an evening for herself.

"Oh no." Allison laughed. "I'm meeting some friends from my book club. There'll be four of us. Actually, here comes Anne now." A moment later, a young woman with blond hair stepped through the door. Allison hugged her.

"A girls' night out. That sounds nice," Hannah said.

"How about we get you set up at this table in the corner?" Elaine led them to a four-top by the front window. The rest of the book club arrived shortly after that, along with other patrons, and soon the dining room was buzzing. It was a good crowd for a Tuesday night, and Raquel and Dylan were busy taking orders, filling water glasses, and chatting with customers.

Hannah saw EMT Brady Flint with his wife and kids. Marshall Fredericks was there again, though alone this time. Hannah suspected that Elaine seated him in Raquel's section on purpose. Liam and Archer walked in, and Elaine led them to the table under the antique fireman's helmet that Liam had donated to decorate the restaurant walls. He caught her eye and smiled as he sat down.

Her heartbeat sped up as she smiled back. He really was very handsome. But he probably smiled at everyone, she told herself. It didn't mean anything.

But a few minutes later, after Dylan had taken their order, she glanced at the table and saw Liam watching her. He didn't look away or even seem embarrassed to be caught. Instead, he grinned at her. Hannah decided to take that as an invitation, so she crossed the room toward the table. Archer spotted her on her way over and elbowed Liam's arm.

"How are you both doing tonight?" Hannah asked.

"Great," Liam said.

"Liam really wanted to come here tonight, so I know he's happy," Archer said. "And if he's happy, I'm happy."

"I've been dreaming about the apple pie I had when I was in here last week," Liam said quickly, and gave Archer a glance she couldn't read. "Is that still on the menu?"

"We baked some fresh this afternoon," Hannah said. "I'm glad to hear it was good enough to bring you back."

"That's not why he's—"

Archer's sentence was cut off sharply by a kick under the table. Hannah pretended she hadn't seen it.

"I've been thinking more about that stuff that was found in the cave on Saturday," Liam said with a glare at his friend. "Have you learned anything more about the guy who left it down there?"

"My dad's uncle Chuck," Hannah said. "I've been trying. We met with his son, Roger, this morning. Everyone thought Chuck died in the cave, but it's looking more and more like he left on purpose and wanted everyone to think he died."

"That's messed up," Archer said. "Why would anyone do something like that?"

"We're not sure yet. It's pretty hard to believe," Hannah said. "But it seems like it's true. What's even crazier is that his son thinks he might have actually met his dad forty-something years later, only his dad didn't reveal who he was."

"What?" Liam said. "That's wild."

"My dad and I thought so too," Hannah said. "Anyway, I'm trying to see if I can track him down. And I'm learning a lot about caving in the process, so there's that."

"You are?" Liam's face brightened.

"I got to see a map of McLeod Cave and where you went." Hannah pulled out her phone and found the photo she'd taken of the map in the guidebook. "See? Here's the entrance, and here's the cavern where Ryder found that stuff."

"Whoa." Liam leaned in. "Can I see?"

She handed him the phone, and he used two fingers to zoom in on the photo. Then he pulled the phone closer.

"As you can see, the place where you rappelled into the cavern isn't marked on the map," Hannah said.

"Because no one knew about it," Archer said. "Ryder and Colt were the first people crazy enough to crawl though the tiny opening to get there, I guess."

"I'd seen that opening before, but I thought it was impassable," Liam said. He was still holding the phone, and it looked like he was typing something, but she couldn't see the screen. "Those guys are insane for trying it."

"But it worked," Archer said, laughing. "People crazy enough to try what no one else does are the ones who make new discoveries."

"Maybe they'll name the passage after them," Liam said, lowering the phone.

"'Ryder and Colt's Scary Descent,'" Hannah said. "It has a nice ring to it."

"It's pretty cool that you got this map," Archer said, taking the phone from Liam so he could see it for himself. "We'll make a caver out of you yet."

"If you're interested, I could take you down there and show you the cavern where the stuff was found," Liam offered. "If that would help you with your mystery."

As much as she liked the idea of spending time with the handsome fire chief—and she couldn't deny that was appealing—not even that was enough to make her agree to the idea of crawling down into that cave.

"I appreciate that you guys enjoy it, but I'm not sure I'm up for that," Hannah said.

She wanted to add that she would be interested in doing something a bit less terrifying—dinner, a movie, a walk in the park—with him instead, if he wanted to, but she couldn't quite bring herself to say the words. What if he didn't feel the same way? What if he was offering the cave thing because he really liked caves, and it had nothing to do with her?

Was she imagining that Liam's smile faltered a bit? Should she say something about seeing him another time? Was that too forward?

"I've got your hot wings," Dylan said, stepping up behind Hannah and sliding the dish onto the table.

"These smell amazing," Archer said, leaning forward.

"They're the best." Liam rubbed his hands together in anticipation.

Dylan confirmed that the firefighters had everything they wanted before hurrying away again.

Her chance to say something about getting together another time was gone. The moment had passed, and Hannah wanted to kick herself. He probably thought she didn't want to hang out with him. What if he thought she wasn't interested? *Was* she interested? Should she have said yes? Why did Dylan have to arrive when he had?

"I'll let you guys enjoy your wings," she said. "Let me know if there's anything else you need."

"Liam needs—"

Whatever Archer was about to say was cut off by another swift kick under the table. Archer started laughing as Hannah walked away. She didn't need someone to kick her. She was kicking herself. That was an opportunity, and she'd blown it. She'd let fear get the best of her, and she didn't know if she'd lost her chance for good.

Several times throughout the next hour, Hannah found her gaze traveling to the table where Liam and Archer sat. It was hard to force herself to look away so she wasn't caught staring, and she was disappointed when they left.

Although there was plenty to keep her busy. Dylan mixed up two orders and dropped a bottle of ketchup that shattered on the dining room floor. He had always been clumsy, but he was so much worse than normal lately. When she had to send out a free dessert for the third time to cover for his errors, she knew she couldn't put the issue off any longer. She needed to address it. Hannah hated having to have conversations about an employee's negative performance. It was the worst part of managing people, but she'd learned from her time in running restaurants in California that she couldn't let things like this go without addressing them. They would only get worse.

Hannah didn't want to interrupt him while they were still serving customers, but once they'd locked the door and were closing down for the night, she pulled Dylan aside and asked him to follow her into the office.

"What's up?" Dylan's eyes were wide. He must have guessed why she'd called him in there.

"You seem distracted recently," Hannah said. "There were three orders that had to be redone tonight. It costs us time, money, and customer goodwill every time that happens. I'm wondering if you can help me understand what's going on."

"I—" Dylan started to say something and then stopped. "I'm sorry," he finally said.

"Is there something I can do to help you?" Hannah tried to be gentle but firm. She had to figure out what he needed to do his job well. "Is there something that's confusing you?"

"I—" he started again, then fell silent.

"You're not in trouble," she said. "I'm just trying to figure out how to fix the problem. I need servers who can deliver the right food to the right table at the right time. I want to make sure you have the support you need to do your job well and feel confident."

Dylan swallowed, closed his eyes, and took a deep breath. Then he opened his eyes and said, "I'm sorry, Hannah. I'll try harder."

She knew he didn't want to go into detail, but she couldn't let him off the hook. She had let this go on far too long as it was. "I appreciate that, but I'd really like to understand what's going on so I can help you."

He stared at her for a long time. Just when she began to think he wouldn't answer, he confessed, "I'm exhausted."

Exhausted? Was that what this was all about? "Is there a reason you're more tired than usual?"

He bit his lip then said, "The truth is, I've been studying a lot. For the SAT. And it's—I guess I've let it get in the way of sleep more than I should have. I really want to do well."

"You're taking the SAT?" Hannah shouldn't have been so surprised. Dylan was a few years out of high school. Why wouldn't he be considering what was next? "Are you thinking about applying to college?"

"I know it's a long shot, so all this studying is probably a waste of time, but I decided I wanted to try, so—"

"Why would you say that?" Hannah said. "What would make it a long shot?"

"I didn't exactly get the best grades in high school," Dylan said. "And my English teacher junior year said I'm probably not college material, so it doesn't seem likely I'll get in."

"Your teacher said that to you?" What kind of teacher said something like that to a student? Teachers were supposed to guide and encourage, not destroy their students' self-esteem.

Dylan avoided her gaze. "Yeah, after I got a D on a paper about *Romeo and Juliet*. He said he'd had freshmen write better papers."

"Oh my goodness. I'm sorry he said that to you. That's horrible, and it was wrong of him." For a moment, Hannah debated tracking down that teacher and giving him a piece of her mind.

But no, that wasn't her place, and it wouldn't undo the damage he'd done. Dylan had taken the cruel words to heart, and they had become self-fulfilling. He believed he wasn't smart enough to go to college, so he hadn't. But now he wanted to, and he deserved the chance like anyone else.

Once her temper was under control, she added, "And I'm sorry this teacher dissuaded you from pursuing college."

"It wasn't only that teacher," Dylan said. "Like I said, my grades weren't the best, so it wasn't like I was ever on the college track, with AP classes and all that. I never took the SAT, and I never applied to college. I started working right after high school, but recently, I've been wondering if that was a mistake."

College wasn't for everyone, for sure. Some of the most successful people in the world hadn't gone to college. Some of the people she loved best, like Dad and Uncle Gordon, had gone to trade school and then went on to have great careers and lives. Not everyone had to get a degree to have a worthwhile career or a good life. But if college—whether at a four-year or two-year school—was something Dylan was interested in, she thought he should go for it.

"So, what changed?" Hannah asked. "What made you decide to try for it now?"

"I don't know," Dylan said. "I guess it's that I don't want to be a server for the rest of my life. No offense."

"None taken," Hannah assured him. "Some people make a career out of serving, but it's not for everyone." Based on what she'd seen, she suspected it wasn't for him long-term. "And I think it's great that you're thinking of your future."

"I'm probably not going to get in," Dylan said.

Hannah remembered feeling that way when she'd decided to apply to college in California. She knew she wanted to cook for a living, but cooking school—and in California no less—seemed so exotic, so unattainable, for a girl from small-town Kentucky. It had felt like her dreams were too big for her reality. But she'd been brave enough to try anyway, and look where she was now.

"I think it's great," she said.

"Thanks, Hannah." A flush crept up his neck.

"Let me know if I can help."

"Okay."

"I do need to ask you to change your study habits so you can get enough sleep to do your job well. I need you to be able to focus while you're here, even if you won't be here forever."

"I hear you," Dylan said. "Loud and clear. I'll do better."

"Thanks, Dylan."

They left the office and joined the rest of the team as they cleaned the dining room and kitchen and got the dishes put away for the night. Hannah's mind spun with all that had happened that day, from the visit to Roger and the revelation about Chuck visiting his son, to the failed conversation with Liam, to the news about Dylan. It had been a full and confusing day.

As she stepped into her apartment that night, her phone beeped with an incoming text.

I ENJOYED DINNER TONIGHT. I ALWAYS ENJOY A VISIT TO YOUR RESTAURANT.

The text had come from Liam "the Brave" Berthold.

She laughed. So that was what he'd been doing with her phone. He'd changed his name in her contacts again. It had been Liam "the Treasure Hunter" Berthold before this.

She reread the message, searching for hidden meanings. He said "her restaurant," not the Hot Spot. He said he'd enjoyed dinner. Did he mean the food, or was there any chance he meant he'd liked seeing her?

Finally, she realized she was overthinking it. Whatever he meant, it had been good to see him, and she was happy that he'd continued the game of changing his name in her phone. For now, she'd focus on that and worry about what the rest of it meant another time.

Chapter Ten

Hannah woke early Wednesday morning and climbed out of bed with a plan. She would see if she could find any information about the three men who had been in Chuck's band. They must have known him pretty well. Plus, if Chuck really had gone on to become a bluegrass musician, it was possible they might know something about him—even if he hadn't kept in touch with them after he left, one of them might have some idea about where she could start searching. Were any of these guys still around?

She also wanted to take a look at Minnie's diaries. She hoped they might tell her something about her life and about what it had been like to be married to Chuck. There might even be a clue in them about what Chuck was thinking in his last days in Blackberry Valley.

But first, coffee. She made a cup and settled down with her Bible. One of her readings came from 2 Timothy 1:7, and she slowly spoke the words out loud. "'For God hath not given us the spirit of fear; but of power, and of love, and of a sound mind.'"

Well, sure, she believed that in her head. She even believed it in her heart. But it was hard to live it sometimes. She didn't want to live in a spirit of fear, but she had to admit, she was afraid of all kinds of things. Of losing Dad like she'd lost Mom. Of her restaurant failing. Of *herself* failing. Of ending up alone. Of risking her heart and having it get broken. And as she'd discovered in the past few days, of caves. Of things that were in caves. Spiders. Bats. Being trapped underground, helpless and waiting for who knew what.

Okay, now she was getting too far into the weeds. The point was, she didn't need to live in fear. She had the power and self-control to live as though she knew the God of the universe personally, because she did. That fact should motivate her every day.

She pushed herself up and got ready for the day, pulling on a cozy wool sweater and jeans. Then she opened her laptop and brought up a search window. She consulted the photo she'd taken of the back of the band picture. *Chuck Lynch, George Grey, Harold Summers, Arturo Vargas, 1957.*

She started by running a search for the name George Grey. Both the first and last names were common enough that they turned up a large number of results, but Hannah couldn't find anyone that resembled the right person. If George Grey was out there, she wasn't finding him.

She tried the name Harold Summers next. She found a social media page for that name and, judging by the profile photo, he could be the right age. He had gray hair and wore a newsboy cap with big glasses. And his location was listed as Cave City, Kentucky. This must be the right person. But the account was private, and Hannah couldn't find any other record of him anywhere online. She sent him a friend request, hoping he might be the kind of person who accepted everyone, but she would have to wait to hear back, or try to track him down some other way.

She turned to the last name on the list, Arturo Vargas. She typed his name into the browser, and the first thing that came up was an obituary in *The Houston Chronicle.* Arturo had died of lung cancer before Hannah was born. He was survived by his wife and three children.

She'd struck out. Well, hopefully the diaries would yield some answers, or at least more leads to explore. She eyed the volumes stacked on her table and decided this would go a lot faster with a friend. She called Lacy.

"Hey," Lacy said when she answered. Hannah heard the soft clucking of chickens on her end of the line. "What's up?"

"I was wondering if you'd have time to help me read some diaries this morning."

"Is this another 'adventure'?"

"Of sorts. Think of it as a literary adventure. A historical one too."

"Now you're scaring me. Whose diaries are we reading?"

Hannah explained about her visit to Roger and the diaries he'd given her.

"I suppose I could spare some time for that."

"I knew you'd be too curious to say no."

Lacy snorted. "You mean I love you too much to say no."

"Whatever. Meet me at Jump Start in half an hour?"

"I'll be there."

Lacy was already seated when Hannah got to Jump Start. "I'll stay as long as I can," she said, gesturing to the empty seat across the small table from her. "I have this restaurant that needs an enormous number of eggs every week, and I have a delivery scheduled for today."

"You don't want to be late for that," Hannah said, grinning. She was proud to use local sources, and Lacy had been supplying the eggs the restaurant needed since they'd opened. "I'll get us some coffee."

Hannah got Lacy a pumpkin spice latte and a regular latte for herself and then sat down and pulled the diaries out of her bag. "This one is from the years leading up to meeting Chuck, and then her marriage and the birth of Roger," she said, holding out a journal covered in black leather. "And this one starts about a year into her marriage, from what I can tell." She indicated a white journal. "Which one do you want?"

"I'll take the earlier one," Lacy said, reaching for the black journal. "What am I looking for exactly?"

"Anything that might be a clue."

"You got it."

Hannah opened the white journal and took a sip of her coffee before she started reading.

June 15, 1959

Chuck came home late last night again. I don't even know what time it was, but it was only a few hours before the baby woke up. He told me he'd been working, which would be funny if it wasn't so ridiculous. Does he think I'm stupid? I know he's out gambling away his paycheck. I'm so sick of this. I don't know how much longer I can take it. I hate to say it, but maybe my mom was right about him.

July 3, 1959

Chuck has a gig tonight in Bowling Green. At least that's what he told me. I'm so tired of questioning his lies. If he comes home with a paycheck, I'll know he was telling the truth—assuming he doesn't lose it in a poker game on the way home.

Roger is in bed, and it's quiet. For a moment, I can almost picture what life would be like without Chuck, which is an awful thing to think, much less write. At least I'd still have Roger, who is the sweetest thing anyone could ever imagine. Everything we've been through has been worth it because of him.

Harold and Nancy invited us over tomorrow for a barbecue. I don't think Chuck realizes how good a friend Harold has been to him. He takes him for granted, just like he takes everyone else for granted.

July 13, 1959

Had a rough night. Roger has a cold and was up for much of the night. Chuck got up once with him. I guess that's better than nothing. He says he's trying. But then this morning, on his day off, he left to explore the cave again. When do I get a day off? What is it about that cave that's more interesting than spending time with his wife and son?

July 18, 1959

Harold came by while Chuck was at work, asking me to pay back the money he lent Chuck last month. I had no idea he'd given Chuck anything and said so. It was more than a hundred dollars, and Chuck told him he needed it to cover a doctor's bill for Roger. This was news to me because I haven't taken Roger to a doctor. Harold was very kind about it, but said he needed the money to pay his parents' rent.

I don't know what Chuck did with the money, but I'm going to find out.

Hannah wondered if Harold was the Harold Summers in the photo with Chuck from 1957. If so, it sounded as if he'd been a close personal friend rather than simply a bandmate.

July 19, 1959

Chuck didn't even act sorry when I asked him about the money. He just said he'd needed it, but wouldn't tell me why. He insisted he'd pay Harold back. I can't believe he would do that to someone he's been friends with since childhood.

Whoever Harold was, Hannah hoped he'd gotten his money before Chuck ran off.

The diary went on in the same manner for several more pages, with Minnie reporting small and large fights between her and Chuck, often about money. What emerged was a picture of Chuck as unreliable and selfish and Minnie questioning the choices she'd made that had gotten her to this point.

But her love for her son was very clear and shone through the pages and the years. Roger was her world. On his first birthday in January 1960, she'd gone on for several paragraphs about everything she loved about her son.

Hannah turned a page, and a small black-and-white photo fell out from between the pages. It was the same photo she'd seen at Roger's home, the studio portrait of Roger in a white striped shirt.

> *June 3, 1960*
>
> *A few weeks ago, Mom and I took Roger to the department store in Bowling Green to get portraits made. We got them back today, and I love them. Isn't he adorable? I had to put some money aside from the cash Chuck gives me each week for groceries, but it was worth it.*

Hannah remembered that at this time married women couldn't have bank accounts or credit cards in their own names. It seemed crazy that it wasn't very long ago when that was true.

The next few months' entries detailed growing tensions between Chuck and Minnie and more times when they were left without money to pay the bills because Chuck lost it gambling.

In July of 1960, Minnie wrote:

> *He has a good job. Working at the farm doesn't pay a lot, but it's enough. Add to that the money he gets from playing gigs, and we should be doing just fine, but instead I'm having to beg my dad for money to cover the rent again. I don't know how much longer I can go on like this.*

And then, in early September 1960, she recounted a fight after failing to make rent once again. *I told him we would be better off without him. It was a horrible thing to say, and I didn't mean to, but once the words were out, I realized they were true.*

The next entry was from November 5, 1960.

I was supposed to meet my sister for dinner tonight, so Chuck was supposed to come home straight after work. He's now two hours late, and I've missed dinner. I'm so mad I almost hope he doesn't come home. I don't know that I can be trusted to not say something I'll regret.

Then, the next day:

November 6, 1960

Chuck didn't come home at all last night. I wonder where he went this time.

There was another entry a few lines later:

It's afternoon now, and he still isn't back, so I started calling around to his friends and over to PJ's Bar. No one has seen him. Part of me wonders if I should be worried, but I'm too mad to be truly concerned yet. Part of me hopes something bad did happen to him. I know that's terrible, but I can't help it.

I called down to the station to report Chuck missing. I'm starting to get nervous. He's never been gone this long. What if something really happened to him?

And then, after a line break, she'd continued in a different color ink:

Walter Knicely called to say Chuck's car is parked by the entrance to the cave on their land. He doesn't know how long it's been there. I called the station to let them know, and they promised to send someone to check it out.

Lawrence from the station just showed up to let me know that Chuck is trapped inside the cave. They went in to see if they could find him and found one of the tunnels collapsed. They think he's on the other side of the collapsed rock, though when they called out to him, he didn't answer. Lawrence wouldn't say they think he might have been crushed by the falling rock, but that's the obvious conclusion. Either that or he's trapped back there. I don't know which is worse.

I feel terrible about all the things I thought about him while I thought he was off gambling.

November 8, 1960

Lawrence says they're sending more rescuers down this morning to try to get Chuck out. I wish I knew why he went to the cave in the first place when he was supposed to come home so I could meet up with my sister. But I know I'm finding something to be angry with him about so I don't feel so guilty.

Lawrence says they're trying, but that the place where the rock collapsed has always been precarious and now they have to be careful or they might bring more rocks down, injuring, or even killing the rescuers. He's been in the cave for two full days by now. If he's still alive, I wonder how much time he has left.

What am I going to do without him? What will happen to Roger and me if he doesn't come back?

November 10, 1960

They're calling off the search. They say it's too dangerous. They didn't come out and say it, but they think there's no chance Chuck is still alive anyway. So that's it.

I'm a widow. Roger has no father. I feel numb. I don't know what to do.

There were several entries in the weeks that followed where Minnie tried to process her grief, shock, and—in her more candid moments—relief. She recounted visits from various family members and friends, including Harold, who offered support however he could. She gave up the apartment and moved back in with her parents. It was interesting to hear all this from her perspective, but there wasn't a lot that seemed new.

"Find anything?" Lacy asked.

"Not really," Hannah admitted, feeling more than a little frustrated. "How about you?"

"I don't think so," Lacy said. "She talks about meeting Chuck in this one, and she's clearly head over heels. He's 'such a talented musician,' and all that. She thinks he's so handsome and calls him her cowboy."

Hannah wrinkled her nose. "He was a farmhand, not a cowboy."

"I know. Maybe it was some kind of inside joke. It's unclear. What is clear is that she thinks he hung the moon. She says they're spending a lot of time together and talks about how her mom warned her to stay away from Chuck because he's no good."

That explained Minnie's later mention of her mother being right after all.

Lacy went on. "Minnie thinks she's wrong, that her mom has never felt like this, doesn't understand what love is—all the predictable things. Then she finds out she's pregnant. Chuck doesn't want to marry her, but her father insists, so they get married. Minnie is starting to have doubts even before the wedding, but she's several months pregnant, so what can she do? They get married and move into a small apartment in town."

"I saw a photo from their wedding yesterday," Hannah said. "They looked happy, at least."

"It seems like they were for a little while. There are a couple of months where she sounds happy enough, but things go bad quickly after the baby is born. That's where this one ends."

"This one picks up soon after that." Hannah closed the journal. "Chuck stayed out late, and he lost a lot of money."

"How?"

"Gambling, I assume. It's not totally clear, but that's what it sounds like. He borrowed money from a friend named Harold and said it was to cover a doctor's bill, but it wasn't, and Minnie doesn't know where it went. That kind of thing."

"Is this Harold guy still around? Maybe you could talk to him."

"I found a social media profile earlier this morning that I think could be him, but it's private," Hannah said. "So I don't know. He could be very much alive and posting every day. Or it could be an account that hasn't been updated in years, if he's passed."

"Do you have a last name?"

"Summers."

Lacy's eyes widened. "That's Lorelai's last name."

"Lorelai Dawson?" She was married to Pastor Bob.

"Yes. Her maiden name is Summers." Lacy picked up her phone and started typing. Hannah leaned over to see what she was doing. "I'm friends with her on this site," Lacy said, tapping on Lorelai's profile picture. "Here it is. Her name is listed as Lorelai Summers Dawson."

"Probably so people who don't know her married name can still find her. Can you tell if she's related to Harold?" Lorelai was in her fifties, if Hannah had to guess, which seemed a little young to be the daughter of a contemporary of Chuck's.

"Let me see." Lacy clicked on Lorelai's friends list and typed in the search bar. "Here's a Harold Summers," she said after a moment. She showed Hannah the screen.

"That's the same profile picture I found this morning," Hannah said.

"We need to talk to her," Lacy said. "She works at Vintage Valley, one of the antique stores downtown."

"Do you have a few minutes for a stop there?"

Lacy checked her phone for the time. "I do have to head back soon, but I guess I could squeeze in a quick trip to look at antiques."

"Sounds like a plan."

"Anything else useful in that journal?" Lacy asked.

"She records his disappearance," Hannah said. "She thought he'd stayed out too late again, but when she realized he was trapped, she was concerned. I really don't think she knew he made it out. She seems convinced he died in the cave."

"That makes sense, considering she had him declared dead and got remarried. She wouldn't have done that if she knew he was alive, right?"

"Right."

Lacy picked up her cup and took a long sip. "As interesting as this is, I need to get back. If we're going to stop at the antique store, we'd better get going."

As they gathered their things to go, Lacy nodded at a corner table. "Your employee is here again."

Hannah looked over and saw that Dylan must have come in while she was absorbed in the diary. He had his book open and was staring at the computer screen with huge headphones on.

Hannah started toward Dylan to say hi.

"Don't go over there and make it weird," Lacy said.

"I won't make it weird. I talked to him last night, and he told me he's studying for the SAT. He wants to apply to college. I want to go encourage him."

"There's a fine line between encouraging and making it weird."

Hannah rolled her eyes and approached Dylan, waving in his line of vision to get his attention.

He slid the headphones down and smiled. "Hey."

"Studying?"

Lacy cleared her throat loudly beside her. And maybe that wasn't the smoothest opening. It was obvious what he was doing.

"Yep. But I slept in, so I promise I'll be alert and doing my best tonight."

"That's good." Hannah ignored Lacy's uncomfortable shifting beside her. "How's it going?"

"It's tough. I'm starting to think maybe my teacher was right when he said I wasn't college material." He laughed, but it sounded hollow.

"He was *not* right," Hannah said firmly. "You can do this, Dylan."

"Thanks." He sighed. "I know I could go to a community college to start, and I wouldn't need to take this crazy test for that. But my dad went to Western Kentucky University, and I've always wanted to go there."

"If you keep working hard, you'll make it."

"Yeah." But he didn't sound like he believed it.

"I think it's really a brave thing to do," Hannah continued. "I wanted to say that in case I didn't last night."

"Thanks." He looked like he was waiting for her to say something more.

"All right, well, it's time for us to go," Lacy said, threading her arm though Hannah's. "Good luck, Dylan."

"Bye." He ducked his head and slipped his headphones back on.

Hannah smiled as she walked away from the table. If Dylan's dedication was anything to go by, he had this test in the bag.

Chapter Eleven

"See? That wasn't weird," Hannah said, following Lacy out of the coffee shop.

They headed down Main Street and turned right. The hills that surrounded the little town were ablaze with orange and gold and red leaves. They were stunning against the cerulean-blue sky.

"It verged on weird," Lacy said. "Anyway, I'm glad to see him try for this. He's had a rough time."

"He has?" Hannah realized she didn't know all that much about Dylan's past.

"Oh yeah. His dad passed away from an aneurysm maybe five years ago or so. He was fine one day and gone the next. Dylan was in high school. Obviously, it was a shock, and Dylan's mom had a tough time of it. She had to go from a part-time to a full-time job, and from what I understand, she was kind of out of it, even when she was around. Grief can be brutal, you know? Anyway, Dylan is the oldest, so he ended up taking care of his younger siblings."

"Really?" That would have happened when Dylan was in his midteens. Hannah couldn't imagine the kind of effect that must have had on him.

"My mom took meals over to the family a few times after he died, so what I know comes from her. I think it's amazing that Dylan is thinking about college now. I don't think it was the difficulty level of the SAT that kept him away before. I think he couldn't leave because there would have been no one to take care of his siblings."

"That's too bad."

"He's a good guy, and he deserves a better hand than he was dealt," Lacy said. "His brother and sister are in high school now, so maybe commuting to college is feasible for him. I don't know. Anyway, now that you know all that, really don't make it weird."

"I would never."

Hannah's phone rang. She pulled it out and saw *Blackberry Valley Public Library* on the screen. She pushed the green icon. "Hello?"

"Hi, Hannah, it's Evangline. I looked into those things I told you I would, and I wanted to let you know what I found out. From what I can tell, there was no circus in town or anywhere near here around the time your great-uncle vanished."

"I suppose that's not a surprise. That theory was always a long shot."

"And I haven't been able to find a bus schedule from that time, though I'll keep trying."

"Thank you, Evangeline. Don't spend too much more time on it."

"All right. Let me know if there's anything else I can do for you."

"Will do. I appreciate it."

Hannah hung up, and as they walked, she filled Lacy in on what Evangline had said. Halfway down the street was the antique store, with a big picture window where a Shaker-style rocking chair piled with cozy quilts was on display.

They walked in, admiring the treasures all around them. A burled oak dresser topped with a large silvered mirror stood nearby.

A stack of old books stood on top of it, next to a porcelain ewer and basin rimmed in gold. Next to that, there was an open steamer trunk piled with linens and a gramophone on a midcentury modern coffee table.

Eventually, they found Lorelai behind the desk.

"Good morning." Lorelai had long hair that was somewhere between blond and white, and stylish glasses. "How are you two this morning?"

"We're doing fine." Hannah didn't know Lorelai well, though she saw her at church every Sunday. From what Hannah could tell, she was always smiling. "How are you?"

"I love this time of year," Lorelai said. "And it's a beautiful day, so I certainly can't complain."

"October is the best," Lacy said.

Hannah agreed, although, truthfully, she had yet to find a season she didn't like in Kentucky. She'd missed the changing seasons living in LA, land of perpetual summer.

"Is there anything I can help you find?" Lorelai asked.

"This is cute," Lacy said, picking up a black beaded flapper dress. She held it against her body. "Too small, sadly."

"When would you wear that?" Hannah asked.

"I don't know. Don't ruin my fun."

"Anyway," Hannah said, turning back to Lorelai, "we're actually not here to shop."

"Though it doesn't mean we won't," Lacy added.

"We wanted to ask you about someone named Harold Summers."

Lorelai tilted her head. "That's my father. What do you want to know about him?"

"We're trying to learn as much as we can about a childhood friend of his, my great-uncle Chuck."

"I don't think I ever heard that name, but you could ask my dad about him."

"Does he live around here?" Hannah asked. Harold's profile had listed his location in Cave City, but that wasn't necessarily accurate.

"He lives in Cave City, in an assisted living place. He has good days and bad days, but he loves visitors, and the past is his favorite subject. Do you want me to call over there and see if he would be willing to talk to you?"

"That'd be great," Hannah said. "Thank you."

"Anytime." Lorelai smiled at her. "Why don't you give me your phone number, and I'll give you a call after I talk with him?"

Hannah gave Lorelai her contact information, and then she and Lacy headed out of the shop. Lacy checked the time again. "Let me know when you hear from her. But I have to get back."

"Thanks for your help."

"You know I wouldn't miss it. I'll see you in a little while when I bring the eggs by."

They walked back to Main Street, where Lacy climbed into her car, and Hannah headed to her apartment. She set the diaries on the table and was trying to decide whether she had time to go to the grocery store when her phone rang. It was a local number, but one she didn't recognize. Normally she'd send it straight to voicemail, but maybe this was an opportunity to practice being brave.

She put the phone to her ear. "Hello?"

"Hi, Hannah. It's Vanessa from down at the station. I have that police file if you want to see it."

"Amazing. I'll be right there."

Sometimes being brave paid off.

Hannah spent the next hour reading through the file in a small conference room at the police station. She read the statement Minnie gave when Chuck disappeared and the notes the officers made about the places they'd gone to look for him on Sunday afternoon—the racetrack in Bowling Green, the venues where he often played, a bar or two. She wrote the names down, but a quick search told her that the bars were no longer in business. Searching for a racetrack in Bowling Green only turned up a track for cars and a go-kart venue.

She read how, at 3:32 p.m. on Sunday, November 6, Minnie called the station to tell them that Walter Knicely had seen Chuck's car by the entrance to the cave. How the officers reported to the cave entrance, went to the Knicely home to use the phone, and called for help from the team of firefighters trained in cave rescues.

There were reports from the days following the discovery that the passageway had collapsed, followed by updates as they tried to get through the fallen rock, culminating in the excruciating decision to cease rescue operations to protect the lives of the rescuers. Even though by that point they were all confident that no crime had been committed, the police file recorded the developments dutifully. But none of it was news to her.

The one thing she found interesting was a note reporting that a week after the search was called off, Minnie called the station again. This time, she called to report that several of Chuck's possessions were missing from the house. Specifically, she couldn't find the silver cuff links he'd received for a wedding gift, the watch he'd inherited from his grandfather, or his fiddle.

Hannah knew what had happened to the watch and the cuff links. They'd been sold, along with his wedding ring, at the pawn shop before he vanished. Minnie wouldn't think to report the wedding ring missing, since she would have assumed he'd been wearing it when he was trapped in the cave. But the fiddle. There was no mention of a fiddle being sold at the pawn shop. It hadn't been in the cave. So where was it?

He must have taken it with him. That was the most obvious answer.

The police had responded to Minnie's call and determined there was no evidence of a break-in. They reported searching for the missing items. But they couldn't have searched all that hard, Hannah thought, or they would have found the watch and cuff links at the pawn shop. There was no record of any of the items ever being discovered.

Hannah left the police station and headed to the restaurant to get to work, even though all she wanted to do was start researching bluegrass bands. If he'd taken his fiddle with him, there really had to be a connection to bluegrass. At last, she had something that felt like a real lead.

She ran upstairs to change and decided she had a few minutes to see whether anything came up in a quick search. She typed in the words *bluegrass band* and *Louisville* and hit return. The first link led to a site for bluegrass fans, and under the *Favorite Bands* tab, there were hundreds of links. Could there really be that many in Louisville alone?

She tried the search again, this time typing in *Lexington* instead of Louisville. She skimmed half a dozen band websites, which were colorful, attractive, and full of information about the bands, such as their members and upcoming concerts. Could any of them be connected to Chuck?

She tried again, searching for *Chuck Lynch* and *bluegrass*. She spent more time than she should have combing through the results, but nothing looked right. Which made sense, since he wasn't using that name. But without his name, how would she find him?

Hannah didn't have time to keep at this. She ran downstairs, unlocked the restaurant, and flipped on the lights, but her mind was still focused on the mystery of what had happened to Chuck. He must have planned to continue playing music when he left.

Where could she find real information about bluegrass musicians? Trying to locate him through a web browser without more specific information was like searching for a needle in a haystack. She chopped peppers and carrots as she thought about the possibilities, pausing only to greet Jacob when he came in. He put his apron on and fell into step around her.

She needed more information to make a search useful. But she didn't have that. Maybe old newspapers would have ads for shows. Or should she start with venues where bluegrass was played back in the sixties and seventies? Maybe the owners had records of bands that had played in those places.

But how would she find those venues? She wasn't even sure which city to focus on—it could be Lexington or Louisville, or maybe even Nashville, since the man Roger talked to said he was going there for a gig. And even if she did find a record of the band names, how could she find out about the people in those bands? How would she know if Chuck was part of one all those years ago if he was living under an assumed name? It felt hopeless.

Soon, though, it was time to open for the night. In no time, they had a good crowd, especially for a Wednesday. Marshall was in Raquel's section again.

"Is he ever going to ask her out?" Elaine said, eyeing them as Raquel took his order.

"You don't think he's here for our great food?" Hannah teased.

"That man has eaten his own weight in wings at this point," Elaine said. "And I don't understand what his hesitation is. She obviously likes him."

Raquel was not merely smiling as she chatted with him at his table. Her whole face seemed to glow. And Marshall grinned at her like a lovesick puppy.

"Maybe he's scared of ruining things if he asks her out and she says no."

"She won't say no." Elaine crossed her arms over her chest. "If he doesn't go for it soon, I may need to nudge things along."

"How would you do that?"

"I don't know yet. But this is getting ridiculous."

Raquel finally stepped away from Marshall. Then she topped off water glasses at two of her other tables, cleared away empty plates at another, and brought out desserts for yet another. She was efficient and focused, even though Hannah could see there was something else on her mind.

Hannah looked over to the other side of the dining room and saw Dylan chatting with an older couple she recognized from church. He hadn't messed up any orders so far tonight, and nothing had been dropped or broken.

Satisfied that all was in order for now, Hannah approached the table in the corner, where newspaper editor Jack Delaney was eating dinner with his wife, and asked how they were enjoying their meal. After she checked on a couple of other customers, her phone buzzed in her pocket.

She pulled it out and saw Lorelai's name. "Hello?"

"Hi, Hannah. It's Lorelai. I spoke with my dad, and he's happy to talk to you about Chuck. He seemed interested to hear what you had to say."

"I'm so glad."

"He asked if you were Gabriel's girl, and when I said yes, he went off on some story about a time your father answered his call in the middle of the night for a burst pipe, and—well, anyway, he's happy to talk to you."

"That's great. Are there certain visiting hours?"

"He tends to do better in the mornings, so I'd go then," Lorelai said. "But any day is good, I think. He's over at Clarkston Commons. Do you need the address?"

Hannah had been there before, visiting Liam's grandfather. "No thank you. I know where it is. Thank you so much for setting this up."

She hung up and put her phone back in her pocket. She would go over in the morning. Maybe Harold would finally be able to give her some answers.

Chapter Twelve

As Hannah drove to Clarkston Commons on Thursday morning, she rehearsed what she was going to say. She would tell Harold what she knew about Chuck's disappearance and what they'd found in the cave. Then she would ask if he had any idea what might have happened to him. It seemed simple enough, especially since Lorelai had already told him why Hannah was coming.

But she had no idea what he might say. What if he'd known the truth about Chuck this whole time? He was Chuck's childhood friend. It was possible he knew something and never told anyone. Or maybe he was as clueless as the rest of them. In any case, she'd find out soon.

Cave City was, as the name implied, the home of many of the area's most well-known underground caverns, including Crystal Onyx Cave, Diamond Cave, and Mammoth Cave National Park. These caves were all show caves, meaning they'd been modified for tourists with staircases and handrails and electric lights. They were nothing like the kind of caving Ryder and Colt and Liam did, exploring unknown and unmapped caverns, but they were as close as Hannah ever wanted to come to underground adventuring.

She parked in front of Clarkston Commons and was greeted by a receptionist whose name tag read RITA.

"Hi, Rita," Hannah said. "I'm here to visit Harold Summers."

"Sure thing. I'll just need you to sign in." Rita pushed a clipboard across the counter toward her. After Hannah signed her name on the line, Rita indicated a hallway to the right. "Harold's room is that way, around the corner."

"Thank you." Hannah made her way through a bright and open atrium then down a tiled hallway lined with rooms. She was pretty sure Patrick Berthold's room was one of these, but she wasn't sure which one, as she'd visited with him in the atrium. She turned the corner and found Harold's room easily enough. The door stood ajar, but Hannah tapped on it anyway.

"Come in," a voice called from inside.

Hannah pushed the door farther open and found a man with white hair sitting in a recliner. He had the same angular face she'd seen in his picture, just more aged, and he smiled at her as she walked in. A bookshelf stuffed with hardbacks was beside his chair, and a parakeet sat in a cage against the far wall.

"You must be Hannah," he said. "Nice to meet you. I'm Harold Summers."

"It's wonderful to meet you," Hannah said.

He gestured to a padded chair beside him, his hand trembling a bit. "Have a seat. You're the spitting image of Elsa, aren't you?"

"I've heard that before." Hannah didn't see it herself, but several other people claimed to, and she took it for the compliment it was. Her grandmother had always been a lovely woman. "Thank you so much for meeting with me."

"I'm glad to have visitors, but I will admit I was especially intrigued when Lorelai told me you asked about Chuck."

"You were childhood friends with him?" Hannah asked.

"Best friends from the time we started kindergarten. He came right up to me on the playground the first day and told me to swing with him, and that was that."

"He didn't ask you? He told you?"

"That was Chuck," Harold said with a chuckle. "He always did know what he wanted, and he knew how to get it."

"I saw that you two were in a band together."

"Oh yes. The Lonesome Canyon Boys. We thought we were something else."

"Lonesome Canyon?"

"There's no such place, of course," Harold said. "We just thought it sounded good. And not to brag, but we were all right, if you'll excuse my saying so. Chuck was more than good though. He was great. I always knew he was going places."

"You played the guitar, right?"

"Yep. And Chuck played the fiddle. George was on bass, and Arturo had the banjo. We played all over town for a while there."

"Did you keep in touch with the other band members?"

"Not really. After Chuck was gone, the whole thing just kind of fell apart. Arturo moved to Houston. George stayed in town, but he got a job in sales. I don't remember exactly what he did, but it was something that meant he was gone a lot, and he wasn't around much after that. He got married, but that didn't last long. He passed a while ago."

"I'm sorry."

He patted her hand. "When you get to be this age, you get used to outliving many of your friends. It doesn't make it easier, but it is what it is. We sure did have some fun back then though. We were—but you didn't come to hear an old man relive his glory days."

"Actually, that's exactly what I came for."

"Nah. You want to know about Chuck. What can I tell you?"

"I'm interested in hearing about when he disappeared, but I'd also love to know a bit more about the time leading up to his disappearance."

"Well, like I said, we were friends starting in kindergarten. We used to run around town getting into all kinds of trouble. Kids were a lot more free back in those days, and we spent hours riding our bikes, sneaking into movies, and exploring in the caves around town."

"You went into the caves by yourselves?"

"Well, together, but without an adult, yes. A lot of kids did. We loved exploring down there. And yes, before you ask, it was dangerous. But like I said, things were different then. Kids had more freedom, more time to explore the world. We learned how to get ourselves out of any mess we got into."

"So Chuck would have been familiar with the entrance to McLeod Cave on Bluegrass Hollow Farm even when he was a kid?"

"Absolutely. We'd been in pretty much all the caves around here by the time we were in high school."

Hannah had suspected as much, based on what he'd already told her. "How did you start playing in a band together?"

"Chuck had dreams of making it as a musician. He probably would have too. He was that good. He organized the group, and we started playing all over."

"It sounds like he really loved music."

"Loved it and was good at it. Aside from his wife and son, I sometimes wondered if it was the only thing he really loved."

"I'd like to know more about his wife and son," Hannah said. "Do you remember when he met Minnie?"

"Boy, do I. She went after him hard."

"Minnie pursued Chuck?"

"She showed up at all his shows and hung around afterward. She made it clear she was interested. Not that it took a lot of convincing. She was older and more sophisticated than girls our age, and it didn't take long before they were together all the time."

"What did you think of her?"

"At first, we all thought she came on a little too strong. But Chuck was impulsive. Always had been. Once his mind was made up about something, that was that. I mean, he was head over heels. We told him we thought things were moving too fast. But he didn't care, and Minnie, like I said, wouldn't let up." He chuckled.

Hannah thought for a moment. "It sounds like Minnie was the leader and Chuck the follower. And yet, in every account I've heard, she comes off as a long-suffering saint married to an unpredictable and, frankly, rather selfish man." Hannah didn't know what she was trying to ask, exactly. Something about whether Minnie could have been in on it, whatever it was, but she didn't even know how to phrase the question.

"Minnie changed when Roger was born," Harold said. "Once she had that baby, he was all that mattered to her. She was a rock while Chuck went off the rails. We should have been warning her about him."

"Tell me about that. His going off the rails, I mean."

"Well, maybe that isn't a fair way to say it. But once she was pregnant and they had to get married, he started to feel trapped, I think. Caught. Like all his dreams of making it big in music just vanished. He was too immature to be a father and a husband, and he knew it."

"Was he acting particularly strange at all before he disappeared?" Hannah asked.

"His behavior was always pretty erratic," Harold said. "Chuck was a lot of things, but measured was not one of them. He was always chasing one thing or another, and he was always all in on whatever he was excited about at the moment. He didn't often see the world like other people, so his actions didn't always make sense to anyone but him. So no, I wouldn't say I noticed any real difference in his behavior."

"I heard that he often stayed out late and that the family struggled with money," Hannah said.

"Both of those things are true," Harold said. "And they're related. Chuck had a good job as a hand on the farm, but he always believed things could change for him. It was his eternal optimism that made him so lovable and at the same time so terrible with money."

"You mean he gambled it away." She'd already heard this from Nana, and Minnie also alluded to it in her diary.

"He was always sure the next race or hand was the one that would turn things around." Harold sighed. "Which often meant that Minnie had to make do at the end of the month."

"I got ahold of Minnie's diary from around this time, and she mentioned that you'd loaned Chuck some money."

"I did. It was foolish of me. I should have known better. He told me Roger was sick and needed a doctor. I couldn't exactly say no to that, though I didn't have much to spare. I was still living at home, but my dad couldn't work. He hadn't been able to since the war. So my mom and my little brothers depended on me. But I gave him the money because he promised to pay it back by the end of the month. He didn't. I suppose it was long gone."

"Did you ever get your money?"

Harold's jaw tightened. "I tried. I hated to go to Minnie and ask for it, but I really needed it. We were behind on our rent because of a real doctor's bill, and I faced the possibility that my parents would be turned out of their home. But Minnie said she didn't have it. They were barely making it themselves. It was a tough time for all of us."

"It sounds like it," Hannah murmured.

"She did eventually pay me back—many years later, when she'd remarried. I appreciated the gesture, though by that point things had stabilized for us."

"I'm glad to hear that," Hannah said. "Can you tell me about when Chuck disappeared?"

"I can tell you what I know. It's not a lot, and it might not be anything new to you if you've read Minnie's diaries. Chuck went down into the caves after work one day."

"Was that strange? For him to go to the cave instead of home after a shift?"

"No," Harold said. "Maybe it should have been, but it wasn't. You understand by now that Chuck was unpredictable. He'd always loved exploring that cave. And since he was already there on the farm for work, he would go in sometimes after his shift. He kept his gear in his car and was able to explore it whenever he wanted to."

"Even though he had a wife and son waiting at home, and he'd been gone all day?"

Harold tapped the side of his nose. "He didn't see it as selfish, of course, but others probably would. The way he saw it, he'd been working all day, and he deserved the chance to do something he loved."

He reached for a cup of water on the small table next to his chair. His hand shook, so Hannah grasped it and handed it to him.

"Thank you." He took a sip.

"You're welcome. So that explains why no one thought it was odd when he went into the cave instead of going home the day he disappeared, I suppose. When did you first hear that he'd gone missing?"

Harold took a long breath, and then he let it out slowly. "I can answer that for you, but first, I have a question for you. You keep saying 'disappeared.' Not 'died.' Why is that?"

Hannah smiled. Harold was still sharp, that was for sure.

"It's because I don't think Harold died in the cave," Hannah said. "I think he made it look like the cave collapsed on him, and then he walked out and started a new life."

"What?" Harold gaped at her. If he'd known about this at the time, he was a very good actor, but Hannah believed his reaction was genuine.

Hannah explained how Ryder and Colt had found Chuck's things in the cavern and what she thought they meant.

"You mean to tell me he didn't die in there, but has been alive this whole time?" Harold demanded.

"I don't know about this whole time," Hannah said. "I don't know what happened to him after he walked out of the cave. I have no idea if he's still around or where he went or anything. But the evidence does seem to indicate that he walked out, made it look like he'd been trapped or killed, and never came back."

Harold was quiet for a long time. Finally, he spoke. "I don't know what to say. If that's true, I'm incredibly disappointed in him."

"So you didn't know?" She was pretty sure she knew the answer, but she still had to ask.

"No. Not a clue. I thought what everyone thought—that he'd died." He was quiet for another moment. "You asked when I learned what had happened. Minnie called me on Sunday, looking for him. Sometime in the afternoon, I think. She said he hadn't come home, and she was hoping he was with me. I told her he wasn't and that I didn't know where he'd gone, which was the truth. We didn't have a gig the night before, so I'd spent the evening at home. The next thing I heard was when Minnie called me that night and said he was in the cave that collapsed."

"So you had no idea this was something he was planning?"

"None at all." He made a face, as if he debated saying something else.

"What is it?"

"I'm not sure it's anything," he said. "Though if it's true, it does explain something."

"What's that?"

Harold pressed his lips together then said, "A few weeks before he died, Chuck stopped me after a gig and asked me to take care of Roger if anything ever happened to him. At the time, I didn't think much of it, though after he died—or after we all thought he died, I guess—I assumed he'd had some kind of eerie premonition. But now I don't think that was it at all."

"He was already planning on leaving."

"I think he must have been. I didn't see it at the time, though that had to have been what he meant." Harold stared down at the cup in his hand. "So what you're telling me is that Chuck faked his own death, walked away from his wife and son, and no one has seen him since?"

"I don't know that it's fair to say that necessarily." She told him about the man who had visited Roger, and what he'd said.

Harold whistled. "Wow. That's some nerve, isn't it?"

"Do you think it could have been him?"

"I think it must have been Chuck. That's exactly the kind of crazy thing he'd do. He probably got a kick out of Roger not knowing who he was. When was this?"

"Roger said it was about fifteen years ago."

"And there's been no trace of him since then?"

"Not that I've been able to find. I guess I was hoping you might have some idea or clue."

"I'm afraid not. I wish I did, but I don't recall any kind of visit or contact from him. Then again, I wasn't looking, was I? I thought he was dead, so I wouldn't have paid attention even if something strange had happened." He sat back in the recliner. "This changes everything, doesn't it? Imagine that. Chuck just walking away from everything he knew."

"It's hard to believe, isn't it?" Hannah tried to think of another word to use, but she couldn't. "It was so selfish of him."

"How so?"

His question startled Hannah. Wasn't it obvious? "Well, to make everyone think you're dead. To waste so many resources on trying to rescue a trapped caver, when he created that collapse himself and wasn't there at all. The rescuers were in danger for days trying to save someone who wasn't even there. And he left his wife and child to fend for themselves while he walked away and started a new life, scot-free."

"I can see how it would appear that way," Harold said slowly. "That's how most people would see it. But I suspect that's not what Chuck thought."

"What else could he have thought?" Hannah asked, genuinely curious. Harold had already admitted that Chuck felt trapped in his life. On the other hand, Chuck was Hannah's relative, and if she could learn something positive about him for once, she was eager to do so. "How else can we interpret his actions?"

"Like I said, Chuck didn't always see the world the way everyone else did. And remember, whatever problems he and Minnie had—problems that were no doubt of his own making—he loved that child more than life itself. He wouldn't have walked away unless he felt he had no choice. Unless he believed there was no better option."

"What do you mean?"

"He wouldn't have left Roger unless he thought it was truly best for the boy."

"You mean he thought leaving his child behind and making him think he was dead was for the best?" It made no sense. The absence of a father was a wound that never truly healed. Roger went on to have a great life, but surely to have known his father—no matter how unreliable he was—would have meant a great deal to him.

"That's my guess. That it was the opposite of selfish, at least the way he saw it. I think he left because he thought it would be the best thing for his son if he was out of the picture. If he truly thought they were better off without him, he might have seen it as the most selfless thing he could do."

Minnie,

I don't think you'll ever see this note, but I feel the need to write it anyway.

I love you. I always will.

I know you won't believe that if you ever find out what I've done, but the truth is, I see how badly I've messed up your life and Roger's, and I know you deserve better. I've tried to be the man you deserve, over and over I've tried, but I keep falling short. I know your life would be better without me in it. I hate that it's true, but it is, and you know it too. If I'm gone, you can move on and give Roger the life he deserves.

I hope you'll never learn what I've done, but if you do, please know that I did it out of love. Please know that I—

Chapter Thirteen

Hannah left Harold's room and started walking back to the entrance, but she saw a familiar face in the hallway ahead of her. Liam. She smiled and hoped her hair looked all right. His face brightened when he saw her.

"Hello." Liam closed the door to the room he'd emerged from. "Fancy meeting you here."

"Hi, Liam. Were you visiting your grandfather?"

"I was."

"How's he doing?" Hannah caught up to him, and together they started toward the entrance.

"He had a good day today. He had a cold last week, but he seems to be over it."

"I'm glad to hear that." Patrick was a nice man, and it was sweet how often Liam visited him.

"And how about you? Here on a visit?" Liam asked.

"Yes, I came to see Harold Summers," Hannah said. "I hadn't met him before, but he was a friend of my great-uncle."

"The cave guy?"

"The cave guy." Hannah nodded. "I was hoping he might be able to tell me something about where my uncle went, but he didn't know."

"I would hope he would have told someone if he had known," Liam said. "Instead of letting everyone believe he was dead."

"Yeah, it would have been pretty hard to keep quiet, but I could see it if he had a good reason," she said. "People keep all kinds of secrets. But he genuinely seems not to know anything. He was as surprised as everyone else to find out Chuck must have made it out of that cave alive."

"I'm sorry you didn't get what you were hoping for." Liam's tone rang with sincerity.

"The truth is out there somewhere. I just have to keep looking."

"What's your theory right now?" They were back in the lobby, and Liam waved goodbye to Rita then held the door open for Hannah. Bright sunshine cast a golden glow over the rolling green hills that surrounded them.

"Well, one of the things that vanished when he went missing was his fiddle. And when he visited his son a few years back, he told him that he was a bluegrass musician."

"Wait. He visited his son?"

"His son didn't know it was him." Hannah told him about the visit Roger had received.

"Whoa. That's very strange," Liam said. "It's sad that your cousin never knew he was talking to his father."

"Definitely. Though if I think about the visit in a more positive light, I can be glad that Chuck never forgot his son and wanted to see him."

"I like how you can find the silver lining," Liam said. "I assume you're trying to figure out if he truly was in a bluegrass band at that point."

"I am, but I'm not having much luck. It's hard enough to find out about the members of present-day bluegrass bands. I can find all kinds of slick websites, but they don't give much information about the members of the band or where they live or anything like that."

"That doesn't surprise me. And you're not necessarily searching for a modern bluegrass band. You're trying to find one that would have been performing fifteen years ago." They started walking across the parking lot to her car.

"Which appears to be pretty impossible."

"Not impossible," Liam said. "You just need the right tools."

"Well, I haven't found those yet."

"Actually, I may have something for you."

Hannah was surprised. "Really?"

"I'm not making any promises, but my dad is really into bluegrass."

"He is?" Liam's father was a retired firefighter who had moved to Florida with his wife when Liam became fire chief. "Does he play an instrument?"

"Well, he followed a bunch of bands and really enjoys that style of music. I'll give him a call and see if he knows the guy. Chuck—what's his last name?"

"Lynch. Though he introduced himself to Roger as Charles, so maybe ask him about that too."

"Okay, I'll see if he knows anything about Chuck or Charles Lynch."

"That would be great. Though I suspect he might be using a different name."

"Do you know what name that would be?"

"Not a clue."

"Well, I'll have him start with the name Chuck or Charles Lynch and see where that gets us. He also subscribed to a bluegrass magazine for basically my whole life. I think he has pretty much every issue that was ever published stashed in his storage unit."

Hannah laughed. "I think you're exaggerating."

"I promise I'm not. In case you hadn't noticed, my family is rife with pack rats. For Gramps, it's antique firehouse memorabilia, and for my dad, it's anything to do with bluegrass. A normal person would have tossed them all when my parents moved away, but Dad couldn't bear to part with them. Or his band posters, or his collection of vintage guitars."

"What about you? What do you collect?" They had reached her car and stood beside it while they continued talking.

"I have so much camping and caving gear I could open my own sporting goods store. I always say I have enough, but then a new clamp, headlamp, or sleeping bag liner comes out, and I realize it's exactly what I've been missing my entire life."

"I suppose there are worse things to collect."

"That's what I tell myself. Do I need three backpacking tents? Probably not. But are there worse things I could be accumulating? For sure."

Hannah couldn't imagine needing even one backpacking tent.

"I'm sure he has copies of *Bluegrass Unlimited* from around the time you're interested in. Dad's storage unit is in town, so I'll go take a look and see if I can find anything."

"That would be great. Thank you."

"Maybe they should call me Liam the Great instead of Liam the Brave."

Hannah laughed. “Someday you’re going to run out of names to call yourself in my phone.”

“But today is not that day.” He grinned at her. “I’ll give you a call about what I find in the storage unit.”

“That sounds good. Thank you.”

“Any time.” He started walking to his car.

Hannah climbed into her own car, no longer thinking about Chuck or bluegrass or anything but what a nice guy Liam was to help her out like this again. He probably did it for everyone—he was that kind of guy—but she couldn’t help but wonder if there was anything more to it than that.

The dinner rush was in full swing, but Hannah’s staff had everything well in hand. Hannah was in the office going over invoices when Raquel poked her head in and told her she had a visitor.

“Liam’s here,” she said with a wink.

“What’s that wink for? Liam’s helping me with something.”

“Right.” Raquel nodded sagely. “Anyway, he’s waiting for you by the hostess stand.”

Trying to ignore the obvious implications, Hannah followed Raquel, who went to go check on her tables while Hannah continued to the front of the dining room. Liam stood in the small waiting area with a dusty cardboard box in his arms.

“Hi. Twice in one day? I’m a lucky girl,” Hannah said, and then wanted to kick herself. *What a corny thing to say.*

"I went by the storage unit this afternoon, and I brought you all the issues of *Bluegrass Unlimited* from about fifteen years ago."

"Thank you. I really appreciate it." She reached out her arms to take the box, but as soon as he let go, she felt how astonishingly heavy it was. She grunted involuntarily.

"Sorry. It's a lot. Here. Let me have it."

Hannah gratefully passed the box back to him.

"Where do you want it?"

"I guess I need to take it to my apartment. Do you mind taking it up?"

"Not at all. Show me the way."

Hannah led him up the stairs, grateful that she wasn't carrying the box. She unlocked the apartment door and pushed it open.

"Wow. You've done great with this," Liam said, following her inside. He looked around. "Way better than when we would hang out here between calls." The Hot Spot itself took up the area that had held the trucks, equipment, and offices for the fire station. What was now Hannah's apartment had been the firefighters' lounge space.

"I'm glad you approve. I know it can be strange to see a place you're familiar with totally changed."

"It is, but in a good way. That's where the couch was," Liam said, pointing to the kitchen. "And we'd make ramen and other delicacies like that on a little stove over there." He gestured to the corner. "Bunk beds were in there." He indicated where her couch was. "It looks so much better. You've made great use of the area. It flows so much nicer, and it's definitely homier."

Hannah was a bit overwhelmed by the compliments. All she could think to say in response was, “Thank you.”

He set the box on the table and lifted out the top issue. The cover featured a faded picture of a band playing under bright overhead lights, partly obscured by headlines. *Bluegrass Unlimited* was at the top. “I don’t know if these will be any help, but here they are. I’d forgotten the magazine is published by the Bluegrass Music Hall of Fame.”

“I didn’t know there was such a thing.”

Liam peered at her over the top of the magazine. “Are you sure you’re really from Kentucky?”

“Pretty sure. But my parents weren’t into bluegrass. Some country, but mostly we listened to Christian music when I was growing up.”

“I guess I can’t say anything bad about that,” Liam said with a grin. “But I do think you might enjoy bluegrass if you tried it.”

“I’ve liked the snippets I’ve heard over the years.”

“Well, you have everything you need to dive into your education right here.” He set the magazine down on top of the pile. “If the answers you’re looking for aren’t in this box, I don’t know where they might be.”

“Thank you. I’ll start going through them tomorrow.”

“No hurry. It’s not like anyone else urgently needs Dad’s old magazines. I didn’t get a chance to talk to him about all this. When I called earlier, he was out helping a neighbor with her roof. But Mom promised to pass along the message and have him call me back. I’ll let you know whether he knows of a Chuck Lynch after I talk to him.”

“I appreciate it. I’m sorry for dumping this project on you. It’s become much larger than I expected.”

He shrugged. “It’s an excuse to call you, so I can’t complain.”

Hannah couldn’t have heard that right. Had he just said he was happy for an excuse to call her? How was she supposed to respond to that? She should probably ignore it. He couldn’t have meant that the way it sounded.

But how else could he have meant it? It sounded almost flirtatious. If she was brave enough, she could flirt right back.

“You know, you don’t need an excuse to call me.” She regretted the words as soon as they were out of her mouth. That was too bold. What was she thinking?

“Is that right?” He lifted his chin and eyed her, one side of his mouth quirked up in a crooked smile.

“If you wanted to. Or if you didn’t have anything better to do or whatever.” What was she saying? She was babbling now, probably scaring him away.

“I’ll keep that in mind,” he said, still smiling as he turned to the door. She was right—she’d scared him off. “I have work to do at the station. I’m on duty tonight, and I know you have to get back to the restaurant. But let me know if you have any questions or if you need anything else.”

“I will.”

“And I’ll give you a call when I talk to my dad.” He hesitated, and then said, “Or, you know, maybe just to say hi.”

Before Hannah could think of how to respond, he went down the stairs, leaving her alone in her apartment. Grinning like an utter fool.

Chapter Fourteen

Friday morning dawned gloomy and wet, with sheets of rain pouring from a heavy gray sky. It was the perfect morning to sit inside under a cozy blanket and read, Hannah reflected as she climbed out of bed. She made a pot of coffee and a big bowl of oatmeal, and she read her Bible and prayed while she ate. Then she poured herself another cup of coffee and settled down on the couch under a soft throw blanket beside the box of magazines Liam had brought her.

The magazine on top of the stack was an issue of *Bluegrass Unlimited* from fifteen years ago. The cover showed a band called Thursday, according to the headline, and featured stories about several other artists Hannah had never heard of. She flipped through the magazine, gazing at each page to see if—well, she didn't really know what she was looking for, but she hoped she would know it when she saw it. She learned about a band that reunited after decades apart, and read a review of a new album by an artist whose name even she recognized. She read about bands called the Country Gentlemen, the Lonesome River Band, Kentucky Thunder, and Old Crow Medicine Show. But she didn't see anything that made her think of Chuck.

She set that issue aside and picked up the next one, which contained more of the same. It was interesting, and she learned of a whole world she knew almost nothing about. But the exercise was not especially helpful in her quest to find Chuck. She supposed she was hoping to learn that he was now headlining his own show or was the frontman for a band. The Chuck Lynch Band or something along those lines. But there was nothing in this issue either. And really, if he was using a fake name—as she'd suspected from the beginning—why would there be? Still, she had to check.

She paged through a dozen more issues. Even if she wasn't learning what she was hoping for, it was a pleasant way to spend a rainy morning. But there were plenty more magazines in the box, and she wondered if it would be worth it to keep going. It seemed less and less likely that she would learn anything this way. She poured herself another cup of coffee and went through a few more issues. She was starting to think about lunch when her phone rang. Liam "the Brave" Berthold.

She answered immediately. "Hello?"

"Hey. I just spoke with my dad. The name Chuck Lynch doesn't ring a bell for him."

"Yeah, I figured he'd be using a different name."

"That would make sense, especially since he left his ID behind. It's easy enough to get a new identity."

"Is it though?"

"At the time it was. Still is, if you know where to look."

"And do you?" she teased. "Know where to look?" What kind of people was he hanging out with, anyway?

"I mean, I don't personally, but I know it can be done, if you really want to. But it was admittedly easier back then, when IDs were just pieces of paper with no picture. You'd pay someone to write out a new birth certificate, and that was that. It's no doubt much harder these days. The technology has advanced a lot, specifically to make this harder to do. But I wouldn't be surprised if he was able to get something convincing without much trouble in 1960."

"Unfortunately, I don't know what name he would have started using."

"That does make it more difficult."

"I know. Thanks for checking. I guess it was always a long shot."

"Hold on, Hannah. He doesn't know the name, but he also said that he doesn't know everyone in bluegrass. He suggested a visit to the Bluegrass Music Hall of Fame. He has a friend who works there, and he'd probably be willing to talk to us."

Hannah tried not to put too much emphasis on his use of *us*. It was probably a simple slip of the tongue. "Where is it?"

"Owensboro, Kentucky, about an hour and a half from here. The magazine is published by the museum. If anyone might know about your great-uncle, it's likely to be someone there."

"I guess so." It sounded like a long drive for probably not much payoff. But if she could learn something about Chuck, it would be worth it.

"I'd be happy to go with you, if you want."

So he had meant to say *us* after all. "Really?"

"Sure. I haven't been in years. My dad took me there once, and it was a nice place. I don't know nearly as much as he does about bluegrass, but I enjoyed it. Besides, I'd be a connection for you, since it's my dad's friend who works there."

"Okay." She wasn't saying yes just because Liam would be going too. Not at all. She might learn something about her missing great-uncle who might be a bluegrass musician.

"Great. I'm off tomorrow. Does that work for you?"

"What time does it open?"

"Just give me a second..." A moment later he said, "The website says ten to five on Saturdays."

She thought about her schedule. "Can we leave early, so we're there as soon as it opens? That way we don't have to rush."

"Of course."

"In that case, it sounds great."

"I'll pick you up first thing in the morning."

Hannah was distracted that afternoon, thinking about her trip to western Kentucky with Liam in the morning, and so it took her a while to realize that Dylan wasn't moving as fast as usual. Maybe that was a good thing. After all, his problem was that he hurried too much, rushing to take orders without recording them correctly, spilling things as he dashed around. But something was off today, again. He'd only rolled up half of the silverware by the time they needed to open the doors. Instead of chastising him, she pulled him aside.

"Hey, Dylan. Is something going on?" she asked.

"I'm sorry," Dylan said. "I didn't realize I was so bad it was noticeable. I'll do better."

"You're not in trouble," Hannah assured him. She wasn't sure it was her place to ask about his activities outside of work. But considering that whatever it was seemed to be affecting his job performance once more, she decided she had the right. He would let her know if she overstepped. "I'm just trying to understand. What's going on? Is it something related to your studies?"

"I'm sorry," Dylan said again. He took a deep breath. "I've been trying really hard to do a good job since you talked to me before, and I hate it that I'm not. Maybe this is just another thing I'm no good at."

Truthfully, Hannah had wondered more than once if Dylan was cut out for waiting tables, but everyone loved him, and she didn't want to think about replacing him unless it was absolutely necessary. But that wasn't what caught her attention in what he'd said.

"What do you mean, 'another thing'?"

"I mean, I've been wondering if my teacher was right. If I'm not college material after all. I guess I've been down about that. I'm sorry it shows. I'll work on—"

"Dylan, listen to me." Hannah rarely got stern with her staff, but she was determined to get through to him. "You cannot let that teacher get into your head. You have what it takes. You can do this, if you keep working at it."

"I took a practice test today, and it was harder than I expected. My score was not what it needs to be."

"So you keep practicing. You keep working. They offer the SAT regularly. If you're not ready for this round, you work toward the next round. You can do this, Dylan."

He avoided her gaze. "I've been thinking it might be better to just apply to community college instead. Maybe that's a more realistic place for me."

"If community college is what you want and what makes sense for you, you should absolutely do that. You can get a great education at a low cost that way. But if you're looking at it because you don't think you're good enough to get into the school you really want to go to, I don't accept that."

It wasn't her place to accept it or not, but she was getting fired up. Who was this teacher, to crush a young man's dreams?

"Even if I do get in by some miracle, all the other students will have come straight from high school. They'll have their families supporting them, and I won't be able to compete."

"I felt the same way when I started at cooking school."

That seemed to snap Dylan out of his spiral of self-pity. His head shot up. "Really?"

"One hundred percent."

"But you're an amazing cook."

"Back then I was just a girl from small-town Kentucky who was completely out of my comfort zone. I was far away from everything and everyone I knew, and I thought all the other students had more experience and must know so much already. I was completely overwhelmed and thought I couldn't do it. I was certain I'd gotten in over my head. Bitten off more than I could chew, if you will." She gave him a small smile.

He snorted at her joke. "So what did you do?"

"I just did it," Hannah told him. "I refused to give up. It was what I wanted, and I was determined not to fail. It was hard at first, but it didn't take me long to realize that everyone else was just as nervous and overwhelmed as I was—even the ones who seemed confident or like they already knew enough to be working in a professional kitchen. It's hard to start something new when you think you might not be able to handle it. But I've known you for a while now, and I believe you can do this."

Dylan looked at her with a dubious expression.

Hannah wished she knew how to encourage him so he would believe it. There were some people who always knew the right thing to say, but she was unfortunately not one of them. All she could do was speak from her heart, so that's what she did. "It takes guts to try for something like this. I'm proud of you for setting a goal and pursuing it. Whatever happens, I'll support you however I can. You can do this, Dylan."

"Thanks, Hannah."

She didn't know if he believed her, but she hoped he did. She hoped that her words of encouragement would drown out the voice that said he couldn't do it. She hoped he would be brave enough to keep trying.

But for now, she hoped he would get back to work.

Chapter Fifteen

Liam texted Hannah at eight thirty on Saturday morning to let her know he was there to pick her up. Hannah ran a brush through her hair one last time, grabbed her bag, and headed down to meet him. She found him leaning against his Jeep, legs crossed, a large cup of coffee in each hand.

He straightened with a smile when she stepped outside. "Good morning. Ready for an epic trip?"

"I don't know about epic, but I'm excited."

"I brought you some coffee. Zane gave me your usual from Jump Start." He offered the cup to her. "And I got some fuel for the road as well. That's in the car."

She accepted the coffee with gratitude. "You are a saint."

He opened the door for her, and then he walked around and climbed into the driver's side.

She settled in the passenger seat. His car was clean, and it smelled nice, like leather and coffee. A bag from Sweet Caroline's Bakery sat on the console between them. She opened it and peeked inside to find several kinds of doughnuts and scones.

"You got enough fuel for an army."

"I wasn't sure what you'd want."

She sorted through the bag and settled on a chocolate-glazed doughnut. "Thank you."

"Good choice." Liam grinned as he buckled his seat belt and started the car. "Do you have a preference for music?"

"I don't know. I almost feel like we should listen to some bluegrass to get us in the right frame of mind to visit the museum."

"That sounds good." He picked up his phone, which was plugged into the dashboard, and used a music app to pull up a bluegrass playlist. "This is called 'Best of Bluegrass.' Sound good?"

"It sounds like exactly what we want."

"I know a bit about bluegrass—I couldn't really help it, given how much my dad likes it—but I don't know nearly as much as I should," Liam admitted.

"Has your father ever played bluegrass?"

"Not that I know of. He plays the guitar, but I never heard him play bluegrass."

"How about you? Do you play any instruments?"

"I dabble in guitar as well, but I'm not a professional or anything. What about you?"

She'd had no idea he had any musical talent. "I played the flute in middle school but gave it up in high school. Lacy was in the marching band, and it always seemed like they had a lot of fun, but I am not coordinated enough to march and play an instrument at the same time."

"I'm still bitter that they didn't want a guitar player," Liam joked. "Not that I would be able to play and march at the same time myself."

Hannah took a bite of the doughnut, savoring how the pillowy treat contrasted with the rich chocolate. "You played football, right?" Liam had been two years ahead of her in school, so they didn't cross paths much, but even back then he was the kind of guy people couldn't help but notice.

"Good memory."

"It wasn't that big a school," Hannah reminded him.

The streets of Blackberry Valley were quiet, with just a few cars out, but the day had dawned clear and bright, and the city seemed swept clean after yesterday's rain.

"You were in student government. I remember that," Liam said.

"You do?"

"I thought you were cute even back then."

Hannah laughed because she didn't know what else to do. It sounded like he meant he still thought she was cute. But she was probably reading into it. Surely he was just being friendly.

"So, Hannah Prentiss. We have a long car ride ahead of us. Tell me about yourself."

"What do you want to know?"

"Best childhood memory."

"Oh, wow. Let me think."

Hannah had had a happy childhood, so there were many options to choose from—camping trips in the summer, county fairs, visits to amusement parks, even a visit to North Carolina and seeing the ocean for the first time when she was ten. But those weren't what really stood out for her.

"Sitting on the back porch with my parents on summer nights, eating ice cream and watching the lightning bugs come out."

"Well, that sounds totally charming. Utterly idyllic."

"That's why it's my favorite. I'm fortunate to have such memories. What about you?"

"It's hard to pick a single moment, but I think it would have to be the first time my dad let me sit in a fire truck. That's when I knew what I wanted to do for the rest of my life."

"That's really sweet." She took a sip of the coffee. It was dark and rich and strong, as she'd come to expect from Jump Start. "Did you ever feel pressured to be a firefighter? With both your dad and your grandpa having been fire chiefs, did you feel you had a choice about what you wanted to do?"

"I definitely had a choice," he reassured her. "My parents were very clear that I could do whatever I wanted. My mom actually begged me not to do it."

"Why?"

"Because it's dangerous, mostly. And because she knew how hard it can be to be married to a firefighter. She wanted something different for me."

"But you did it anyway."

"There was never anything else I wanted to do. I like helping people. And nothing else gives me the satisfaction of rushing into a bad situation and making it better. What about you? Did you always want to be a chef?"

"When I was very young, I wanted to work in a pet store." Hannah chuckled. "I thought playing with kittens all day sounded like a dream come true."

"Nothing wrong with that logic."

"But then I started watching cooking shows on TV when I was around nine or ten, and something about it resonated with me. I would try to copy what I saw, and then I started making dinners for my parents. While I was following other people's recipes, I began to think of ways to improve them. The next thing I knew, I was experimenting with my own recipes. That's when I really started thinking about it as a career."

"I bet your parents loved that." Liam sounded like he meant it.

"They never complained about my interest in cooking, that's for sure. Even when I served something I thought was exciting and it ended up being gross instead."

Liam laughed before asking her about her hobbies, her idea of a perfect vacation, and her favorite flavor of ice cream. Before she knew it, they'd pulled into the parking lot at the Bluegrass Music Hall of Fame. It was a curved glass-fronted building, grand and beautiful. They bought tickets and wandered through the displays of costumes, instruments, record covers, and memorabilia from different eras in bluegrass history. There were videos of famous performances and posters that explained important elements of the musical style.

But none of it gave her any clue about whether Chuck was among the members of any of the bands.

"My dad's friend Brian said he would be around this morning," Liam said. "Let's go see if we can find him."

He led her back through the museum and asked at the front desk if Brian was around.

"I'll go see." The receptionist disappeared, and a few minutes later she led a man in khakis and a button-down shirt out to meet them.

"Liam Berthold. Good to see you. How's your dad?" Brian looked to be in his forties and had thinning light brown hair and glasses.

"He's doing well. Thanks so much for meeting us." Liam shook Brian's hand. "This is Hannah Prentiss."

"Great to meet you."

Hannah shook his hand, and Brian said, "So I hear you want to learn about a bluegrass musician. What's the name?"

"I'm trying to find out about a man named Chuck Lynch," Hannah said. "Or maybe Charles."

"Chuck Lynch?" He muttered the name to himself. "Doesn't ring a bell."

"He would be in his eighties by now," Hannah said. "He was born in 1940. We think he was a bluegrass musician fifteen years ago, at least. If that helps at all."

"That doesn't narrow it down as much as you'd think," Brian said. "I don't recall anyone by that name, but if you'll wait a moment, I'll go take a look in the office and see if I can find any record of him."

"Thank you," Liam said.

While he was gone, Hannah studied the display in front of her, a collection of record album covers through the decades.

"Look at that hair," Liam said, pointing at an album that had to be from the eighties, given the height on the woman's hair and the mustache and sideburns worn by the man.

"There could be a whole display about mustaches through the decades," Hannah said. It was interesting to see how styles and fashions had evolved through the years.

"I don't think I could pull off this one," Liam said, indicating a particularly impressive handlebar mustache.

"So few can," Hannah said consolingly.

They were still chuckling when Brian returned. "No luck, I'm afraid," he said.

Hannah felt her hope evaporate. "You're sure?"

"He doesn't show up in the archive at all. Is there another name he could have used?"

"Probably," Hannah said. "We just don't know what it is."

"Unfortunately, I can't do much with that," Brian told her. "Was he in a band? Do you know what the band name might be?"

"Not a clue. He was in a band called the Lonesome Canyon Boys at one point, but I think that band broke up when he—well, around 1960, I guess." Hannah couldn't bring herself to go into the whole tale at the moment.

Brian had never heard of the Lonesome Canyon Boys. He asked a few more questions, clearly trying to be helpful, but there obviously wasn't a lot more he could tell them. He apologized, and Hannah and Liam said goodbye and wandered out to one of the galleries.

"Maybe he wasn't a bluegrass musician at all after he went away," Hannah said. "Maybe that was what he said to Roger, but it wasn't true. Maybe he never took it up again after the Lonesome Canyon Boys. Or maybe the man who came to see Roger wasn't his father at all, but a stranger who actually needed to use the phone."

"Maybe," Liam said. But she could tell he didn't believe it, and truthfully, neither did she. After all, Roger had checked his call log, and the stranger hadn't made a call.

"If he's using a different name, how in the world would we figure out what that is?" Hannah said.

"I have no idea." Liam gestured around the room. "Do you see him on any of these album covers?"

"Goodness. I wouldn't know." She looked back at the wall of albums. "I've seen photos of him when he was young, in 1960, but I don't know that I'd be able to pick him out if he's on one of these."

"Especially behind all that facial hair," Liam added, smiling.

Nevertheless, she studied the pictures on the wall, examining each face for any resemblance to a young Chuck Lynch, before finally giving up. This was hopeless. Even if he was here, how would she be able to tell? He would have aged decades since the photos she'd seen. "I don't know."

"That's okay," Liam said. "We'll figure it out."

We. She liked the sound of that.

"Let's see what's in here," Liam said. He started to walk into the next room. "This is called the 'Festival Era' section."

The walls were covered with large collages of photographs of every make and model of bluegrass musician. Singles, duos, groups, all picking and sawing away, some to crowds of what looked like thousands. The caption under the largest photo informed Hannah that this room covered the time when bluegrass festivals were popular, from the 1960s to the 1990s.

"This is interesting," Liam said. He was looking at pictures on the far wall from the entrance.

Hannah walked over to see what he was talking about. He pointed to a picture, and she leaned closer to read the caption under it. It took her a minute to understand what he was getting at. At first, nothing about the band name seemed all that interesting.

But a moment later, she saw it. And suddenly, she realized they might have found a clue.

Chapter Sixteen

"The Boneyard Blues," Hannah said. "That's a caving term, isn't it?"

"It is," Liam said. "How did you know that?"

"I read a book about it," Hannah said. "I was trying to understand why anyone in their right mind would wander around in underground caves."

"Fair enough." Liam laughed.

"The section where Ryder found Chuck's things was called a boneyard in one of the articles I read."

"Oh." Liam's eyes widened. "Yes, that would make sense. That room did have some interesting formations, now that I think about it."

"It could be a coincidence." But Hannah didn't think it was. There was a thrum in her veins, a feeling that this was important, that it had to be connected. She was already pulling out her phone to look up the name of the band. She found a site with a photo of five people holding various instruments—a guitar, a mandolin, a bass, a banjo, and a fiddle. Hannah used two fingers to enlarge the photo of the man holding the fiddle. He was older, with wispy white hair, rounded cheeks, and dark glasses.

"Is that him?"

"I don't know," Hannah said. "I only saw a few pictures of him, and he was sixty years younger. It could be him, but I can't be sure."

"Listen to this." Hannah looked over and saw that Liam had pulled up a website on the band on his phone. "This says the band has been around since 1964 and two of the members are original to the band. It was formed in Louisville and has been playing all over the country ever since."

"Does it tell you the name of the band members?"

"Hang on." He scrolled down the screen. "The original members were Ralph Granger on banjo, Ricky Dubois on mandolin, Michael Frank on bass, Hans Reich on guitar, Wayne Miller on fiddle, and Robert Raybuck on banjo."

The fiddler's name caught Hannah's attention. "Wayne Miller?"

"Could that be your great-uncle?"

"I don't know." He could be using any name. She didn't know of a connection to that particular name. "Are there any other pictures?"

Liam kept scrolling down the page. After a moment he held out his phone with a vintage photo on the screen. "This is the band in 1964. Is that him?" He pointed at the fiddler.

Hannah took the phone and zoomed in. The man was thin and wiry, like Chuck had been, but his bushy beard and mustache hid much of his face, so it was hard to tell. She took out her phone and pulled up the pictures she'd taken of the old photos from Roger's box.

"They could be the same person," she said.

"I think they might be," Liam agreed.

"We might be able to figure it out for sure." Once she thought of it, it was obvious. "I'll send Roger a link to the band's website. He'll be able to tell us if it's the same man who came to his door." She emailed the link to Roger along with an explanation. "We'll see what he says. I hope he checks his email soon."

"You could show the 1964 band photo to your grandma, couldn't you?" Liam suggested. "She might be able to tell if it's her brother or not."

"You're right. Why didn't I think of that?"

"This is why they say two heads are better than one. Should we go ask her?" Liam suggested. "You said they live in Cave City, right?" She'd told him more about her grandparents on the drive over.

"I did."

"That's practically on the way home. And I'd like to meet your grandparents anyway."

Hannah tried not to read into that. "Fair warning—my nana's got a strange sense of humor."

"Don't worry. Grandparents love me." He gave her his most charming smile. She had no doubt he was right. He was handsome, brave, charming, and kind. What was not to like?

Hannah called her grandparents to make sure they were home and up for a visit. Before they got on the road, they bought some sandwiches from a nearby restaurant and ate them in the small park across from the museum. Then they got back into Liam's Jeep.

"You want to put their address into the GPS?" Liam asked as they climbed in.

Hannah took his phone and typed in her grandparents' address, and a moment later the screen showed the route to their place.

"So," Liam said as he merged back onto the highway. "I've been thinking."

"About what?"

"About you."

She felt her heartbeat speed up. He was thinking about her?

"And about caves."

Oh. That was less exciting. She tried to hide her disappointment. "What about me and caves?"

"I was thinking I need to get you into one."

"Why?" she asked. "I'll have you know I've been alive for over thirty years without setting foot in a creepy, slimy hole underground, and I'm quite happy about that."

"They're not all slimy," he protested.

"The ones I've read about have super high humidity, which in my experience leads to slime," she replied.

"Okay, so here's why I want to take you into a cave. You obviously think of them as terrifying places."

"Accurately, I might add."

"I'd love to show you a different side of caves."

She raised an eyebrow. "The kinder, gentler side of caves?"

He gave her a wry grin. "The amazing, shockingly beautiful way underground caves reveal the fingerprints of the Creator."

"Oh. When you say it like that, it's really hard to say no without sounding rude."

"What is it you're afraid of, exactly?"

"Um, let's see." She ticked off reasons on her fingers. "Getting trapped underground and dying. The complete dark created by a lack of sunlight. Creepy-crawly creatures. Bats. Claustrophobia. Other cavers, because anyone who intentionally does this is probably deranged. Do you want me to go on?"

"Do you trust me?" Liam asked. His tone was still light, but she thought she detected a serious note beneath the humor.

Hannah didn't know how to respond to that. He was certainly experienced. He had explored caves all over the area and come out alive from all of them. He was even trained in cave rescues. He was someone they called when a person in the caves needed help. He was a firefighter, for heaven's sake. He rescued people for a living.

"I do," she said.

"I would never put you in danger, Hannah," he said. "And I would like to show you one of my favorite places in all of Blackberry Valley."

"I'm guessing it's not the Hot Spot?"

"That's my other favorite place. But this place is really special. And I'd like to show it to you."

Hannah thought about it. She pictured the opening to the cave on Lacy's property, with its dark and steep entryway. Her throat started to close up, and she found it hard to breathe. "It's not the cave Ryder and Colt explored, is it?"

"No, it's not. It's a very easy cave to navigate, perfect for beginners. And the payoff is worth it."

"Are there any scary descents?"

He laughed. "You will not have to rappel into anything. There's one tight squeeze, but you're small enough that you won't have any problem with it."

She thought about it a bit more. She absolutely did not want to go exploring in an underground cave.

But a small part of her did think exploring in an underground cave with Liam would be bearable, if not enjoyable. She liked the idea of spending more time with him. "You promise you're not just trying to scare me to death?"

"I would never do that," Liam said. "I don't think that kind of thing is funny. I genuinely want to share something I enjoy with you, because I think if you give it a chance, you might enjoy it too. I'll be with you every step of the way."

"Okay then. I'll try it."

Liam grinned. "You won't regret it."

"I'm not convinced of that, but I'm willing to give it a shot."

"When can you go?"

"Better go sooner rather than later so I don't change my mind. How about tomorrow after church?"

"That's perfect."

As they drove, Hannah wondered what she'd gotten herself into. Fortunately, it wasn't too much longer before they pulled off the highway and made their way through the streets of the development to Nana and Grandpa's house. Liam followed her as she made her way to the door and rang the bell.

A moment later, Nana opened the door. "Hi, Hannah," she said, her smile spreading across her face. "It's great to see you." She smiled a welcome at Liam. "Hello. I'm Hannah's grandmother, Elsa."

"Liam Berthold," he said. "Pleased to meet you."

"Berthold? Are you related to Bridget Berthold?" Nana asked.

"That's my grandmother," Liam said.

"We used to live in Blackberry Valley, back before we moved here, and I stopped by the library all the time when my kids were young. She had so much patience with them, even when they pulled all the books off the shelves and made too much noise."

"That's what kids do," Liam said. "How can someone get mad about that?"

"Well, not everyone feels that way, but I always appreciated her for it. Your grandmother was a wonderful woman," Nana said.

Grandpa came into the room a moment later, holding a cup of coffee and the newspaper. "Hey, Hannah. And who's this?"

"This is Liam Berthold. He's the Blackberry Valley fire chief."

"Patrick's grandson." Grandpa set his coffee cup on the table and held out his hand. "I'd heard you made fire chief. Congratulations."

"Thank you, sir." Liam shook hands with her grandfather.

"Patrick was so proud when you joined the squad."

"Thank you. That's nice to hear."

"Wouldn't shut up about it, actually," Grandpa said. "A person would think you'd been elected president or something."

"Gene." Nana swatted at him. "Be nice. It's a big accomplishment, worth talking about. Not many people are willing to risk their lives in the course of duty like that. Patrick was understandably proud that his grandson was one of them."

"Anyway, it's nice to meet you." Grandpa made a show of appraising Liam. "You're a good-looking one, aren't you? Not as handsome as I was back in the day, but still pretty handsome." He raised an eyebrow at Hannah. "Is that why he's here?"

"Gene, behave," Nana scolded.

Hannah felt her cheeks go pink, but Liam laughed. "Actually, I'm here because I'm helping Hannah with a project."

"Liam gave me a ride to the Bluegrass Music Hall of Fame this morning," Hannah added, wishing she could sink into the floor.

"Well, that's nice." Nana ushered them into the living room and gestured for them to sit on the couch. "What prompted that?"

Hannah told her grandparents about her trip to visit Roger and about the mysterious man who had stopped by his home fifteen years before.

"Roger doesn't know for sure it was Chuck," she said. "But he had this feeling about the man. It didn't make sense, because he thought his father was dead, but when I told him Chuck didn't die in that cave after all, he mentioned that incident right away."

"Chuck." Nana shook her head. "That would be just like him. He probably got a real kick out of that."

"You always said he loved that boy," Grandpa said. "If there was any reason for him to show up again, it makes sense that it would be for Roger."

"I bet he wanted to meet him, after all that time," Nana said.

"While he was there, he told Roger that he was a bluegrass musician," Hannah said. "And I read in the police report that Chuck's fiddle was missing—"

"It was?" Nana interrupted, surprised.

Hannah nodded. "Minnie mentioned it, among several other items that were missing from his things after he disappeared. The other things were sold at a pawn shop, but as far as we know, the fiddle was never found. So it kind of makes sense, if he ended up moving to Louisville and becoming a musician. Though I couldn't find any musician with the name Chuck Lynch."

"We went to the Bluegrass Music Hall of Fame to see if anyone there could tell us anything about him," Liam said. "But they'd never heard of a bluegrass musician with that name."

"No, I suppose they wouldn't have. He would have changed his name, right?" Nana asked. "I mean, that would be my assumption, since he left his ID in the cave."

"We think he must have," Hannah agreed. "But while we were there, we did come across the name of a band called Boneyard Blues."

"Boneyard? Like a graveyard?" Nana asked.

"That's quite a gruesome name, isn't it?" Grandpa wrinkled his nose.

"It's a caving term," Liam explained. "It refers to a place where water has worn holes in the limestone, and it ends up resembling bones."

"I've only heard it used in reference to cemeteries," Nana said. "I had no idea."

"We don't really know what was intended with this band name," Hannah said. "But given that Uncle Chuck liked caving, and that the part of the cave where his things were found was a boneyard, we thought there might be a connection. So we researched the band, and we found out that it's been around since the 1960s. There's information about them online, but it says the fiddle player's name is Wayne Miller."

Nana gasped. "Wayne was our dad's middle name. And Miller was our great-grandmother's maiden name."

It was exactly the kind of information Hannah hoped her grandmother would be able to provide. The connection was too strong to be a coincidence. That name couldn't be an accident.

"We found photos of the band members online," Liam said.

"That's right." Hannah pulled up the website on her phone and held it out so Nana could take a look. "Can you tell if that fiddle player is Chuck?"

Nana took the phone and peered down at the screen. "I'm not sure, but it could be. Do you have any other pictures?"

"Hang on." Hannah started searching for more photos online.

"Wait. Maybe I have something here," Liam said. "I searched the archive of the *Bluegrass Unlimited* magazine, and I found this article. It's about the band. Here's a picture of the fiddle player."

He held out his phone. They all leaned close to see the photo of a man with a beard and glasses sitting in front of a bookshelf, holding a fiddle. He was much older than he'd been in the previous photo, but it was the same guy.

"The facial hair makes it tricky," Nana said. "If it weren't for the beard, I'd be able to tell for sure."

If it was Chuck, that was probably exactly why he'd grown a beard. But Hannah saw something else. "Look at this." She pointed to a small, framed photo on the bookshelf behind the fiddle player. She could barely make out that it was a photograph of a small boy.

But she recognized it immediately. She'd seen the photo before.

"I know that photograph. It's Roger."

Nana put a hand to her mouth. "Could I see it?"

Liam handed her his phone, and Nana zoomed in on the fiddler's face and then the photograph on the shelf behind him.

"I can't believe it," she whispered. "It's really him. That's Chuck."

Chapter Seventeen

At first, they all sat in stunned silence after Nana identified her long-lost brother in the photograph. Then Liam pulled up the band's website, and they learned that Wayne was still performing with them.

It was crazy to find him like this after all this time. Would he want to hear from them? Who would call Roger and let him know?

"I just can't believe it," Nana kept saying over and over. "I thought he was dead. All these years, I thought he was dead. And here he is, alive."

"And playing bluegrass, apparently," Grandpa added.

"I don't know why we never thought to wonder if he was playing music out there somewhere," Nana said. "Now that I know that, it should have been obvious. What else would he be doing?"

"You didn't think to wonder, because you thought he was dead," Hannah reminded her. "He wanted you to think that. Of course it wouldn't occur to you that he might be out there playing music from beyond the grave,"

"I suppose you're right," Nana said. "But I still feel like I should have known. My own brother." She laughed again. "I just can't believe he's alive. I'd better call Roger and fill him in. Hannah, Liam, you're welcome to stay while I do that."

"Unfortunately, I can't," Hannah said with true regret, checking the time. "I have to get back to the Hot Spot."

"I should get back as well," Liam added.

Hannah promised to check in later to find out how Nana and Roger wanted to proceed. As far as Hannah was concerned, it was up to the two of them. Whether they wanted to reach out to Chuck—now Wayne—or let him stay a mystery in all their minds.

Hannah certainly hoped they would choose to meet him, to ask him why he'd done what he did. She wanted answers. Accountability, even. Chuck had caused so much heartbreak, making everyone think he was dead. He ran away from his wife and son. Hannah wanted to know why.

Back at the Hot Spot, Hannah stopped at the bottom of the stairs. "Thanks for running me all over the place today," she said to Liam. "I hope it wasn't too much."

"Are you kidding? This is the best day I've spent in a long time," he said, grinning. "Too bad it's probably going to be surpassed by tomorrow."

She'd momentarily forgotten that she had promised to go into a cave with him. What had she been thinking?

"Do I need to bring anything?"

"Nope. You'll want to change after church. You probably don't want to go caving in nice clothes. But that's it."

"All right. I guess I'll see you then."

Hannah was filled with plenty of confusing emotions as she made her way up the stairs to her apartment—dread, excitement, wonder, confusion, anticipation. Hope. It had been a great day, and not just because they'd found out where Uncle Chuck was. It had been great to do it all with Liam. She wondered if he felt the same way.

But she didn't have time to worry about that now. The restaurant would open soon, and it would likely be a busy night. After she took a few minutes to freshen up, she went downstairs and saw that everything looked ready to go. Elaine stood behind the hostess stand, checking that she had the menus and silverware rolls stacked. Dylan and Raquel lit the small votive candles on the tables. The smell of bacon and cooking chicken filled the dining room, which meant Jacob was ready in the back.

"Everything's set, boss," Elaine said, saluting Hannah.

Hannah laughed and unlocked the doors. Once again, she was thankful she had such a capable staff. The first few groups filed in, and soon the room was filled with laughter and conversation, and the smells emanating from the kitchen only improved when the first slices of Jacob's pumpkin cheesecake came out for dessert.

It was a busy Saturday evening. Evelyn and Gretta from church were there, as well as Kylie Jacobs and her father, and Karen DiSalvo and her husband. And there, at the same table as last night, was Marshall Fredericks.

"Think he'll work up the courage to ask her tonight?" Elaine asked, smiling. She'd evidently seen where Hannah's gaze had fallen.

"I hope so, for his sake. He's going to go broke eating here every night if it takes him much longer," Hannah said.

"He's a nice kid," Elaine said. "But I don't see why he's hesitating. It's obvious she likes him. She's going to say yes."

"Maybe we should have slipped him a note telling him that inside his menu?" Hannah suggested.

"Sadly, I think that would be crossing a line, but I'm tempted. If he comes in here with that lovesick puppy dog face one more time without asking her out, I may not be able to restrain myself."

Elaine and Hannah watched as Raquel walked over to fill Marshall's water glass. His face lit up, and Raquel smiled as she spoke to him. Although Hannah couldn't hear what they were saying, it was clear there was a flirty air between them.

Hannah looked around the room and saw Dylan chatting with Evelyn and Gretta. She didn't know how long the two of them had been best friends, but it had been many decades. They both seemed charmed by Dylan's slightly clumsy manner.

"He reminds them of their grandkids," Elaine said, nodding at the table.

"You think?"

"Just a guess, but I bet they tip him well."

"Let's hope so." Now that Hannah knew what he was saving up for, she wanted him to get as many big tips as he could.

"There's something different about him today," Elaine said. "He seems more settled somehow."

Hannah couldn't see it. Still, she trusted Elaine's judgment. Her hostess saw everything, and she knew how to read people better than most.

"I wonder if he's got a girlfriend," Elaine said.

"I don't know." It wasn't her place to share what she knew.

"Oh, boy. Here comes trouble," Elaine said, and Hannah laughed when she saw Elaine's son, Blake, and a few friends coming through the door. "He's home for fall break and has been out with his friends almost since the minute he got home."

Soon the dinner rush was in full swing, and Hannah stepped in to carry dishes to tables and refill water glasses when Dylan and Raquel struggled to keep up. It was hard work, but it was wonderful to see her restaurant full of so many happy people.

Around seven o'clock there was a bit of a lull, and Hannah decided to take advantage of a quiet moment to pull Dylan aside. She caught him near the beverage stand.

"Dylan, you're doing a great job tonight," she said to him. "Elaine even noticed there was something different about you. I just wanted to say I noticed, and to keep it up."

"Thanks." Dylan's cheeks flushed. He stood there, working his mouth as if debating whether to say something else. Finally, he asked, "How did you do it? Make it through cooking school, I mean, when everyone else was better qualified?"

Hannah was surprised by the question, but she tried not to show it. She took a deep breath before she answered. "Well, for starters, I realized they only *seemed* more qualified. That part was all in my head."

Dylan looked confused, so she explained. "Most of them had about as much experience as I did, even if their résumés were more impressive. Once we got into the kitchen, I realized that I could hold my own. I could chop and dice and sear just as well as they could. And they were every bit as nervous as I was. Most of them were just acting like they knew what they were doing."

"Really?"

Raquel walked up to refill a water pitcher, but Hannah continued. It didn't matter if Raquel overheard her talking about her cooking school days.

"Really. They were as afraid as I was most of the time," Hannah said. "And the other thing was that I decided I might fail, but it wouldn't kill me if I did. Once I realized that failure wasn't the worst thing that could happen—giving up without giving it my best was way worse—it was easier to put myself out there and really go for it."

"Okay." Dylan nodded, like he was soaking it all in. "Failure won't kill me," he said under his breath.

"Failure would feel bad for a little while. But it's better than not taking the chance and always wondering what might have happened if you'd been brave enough to do it," Hannah said.

Raquel had finished filling the water pitcher, but she hovered, and Hannah could tell she was listening.

"All right," Dylan said. "I can be brave."

"I know you can."

"You know what?" Raquel set down the pitcher. "You're totally right. The possibility of failing is worse than never knowing."

"Exactly," Hannah said, but now it was her turn to be confused. Raquel agreed with what she'd said, but she wasn't talking to Dylan. Instead, she seemed to be talking to herself.

"I'm going to be brave too," Raquel said. And then, before Hannah knew what was happening, the young woman strode off across the dining room. Hannah looked at Dylan, who shrugged, and then they both turned back to watch Raquel as she walked up to the table where Marshall lingered over his dessert.

"Marshall," Raquel said loudly enough that everyone in the restaurant could hear, "I like it that you come in here most nights. I like seeing you here. But I'd also like to see you outside of here too. So I was wondering—would you go out with me sometime?"

Marshall's eyes widened. He appeared to be at a loss for words for a moment before he stammered, "Y-yes, I would like that very much."

"Great," Raquel said firmly. "Now, can I get you anything else?"

"No," Marshall said, and a smile spread across his face. "No, I think I have everything I came in here for."

The noise of the dining room covered up whatever it was Raquel said next, and Hannah realized she needed to get back to work. Dylan still stood beside her with his mouth hanging open.

"See?" Hannah said. "Sometimes being brave pays off."

Chapter Eighteen

When Hannah got home Saturday night, she dug through the box of *Bluegrass Unlimited* magazines until she found the one that featured the article about Boneyard Blues they'd found online. The tiny photo of Roger in the background was more noticeable and clear in print, and she knew for certain they'd found the right guy.

Hannah also flipped through other issues of the magazine. Now that she knew what she was looking for, she found mentions of the band in several of them. They seemed to be well known in bluegrass circles and to have achieved some measure of success.

So how would Wayne Miller respond to an invitation to connect to his less-successful past?

Hannah went to bed feeling pleased with the progress they'd made, but she didn't sleep well. Her rest was marred by anxious dreams about getting stuck in a cave. When she awoke on Sunday morning, she seriously considered texting Liam and calling it off. He would understand, wouldn't he?

But when she thought back to what she'd told Dylan about bravery the night before, she knew she couldn't do it. She had to go through with this, no matter how afraid she was. She prayed as she got ready for church, asking the Lord for courage and strength. At church, she greeted her friends and family and sat through the service, trying to act like everything was normal. But inside, she hoped for an earthquake to strike—though they didn't even have earthquakes in Kentucky—or a massive fire that would require all firefighters, even those who were off-duty, to show up and help. One where no one got hurt, of course.

"Do you want to come over for lunch?" Lacy asked as they walked out of the church building together.

"I can't, sadly. I'm going caving with Liam."

Lacy blinked. "I'm sorry, I must have misheard you. I thought you just told me you were going caving with Liam."

"That's what I said."

"Okay, I apparently missed some major developments in your life."

"There are no major developments. I'm pretty sure he's going to get me killed."

Lacy didn't take the bait. "Which cave are you going to?"

"I don't know. Not the one on your property though. He said it's one that's good for beginners. I should probably find out so you know where to look for my body—"

Lacy cut her off in a clear refusal to be distracted. "When did this happen?"

"Yesterday, when we drove back from the Bluegrass Music Hall of Fame."

"I'm sorry, what?" Lacy's mouth dropped open. "You went there with Liam and didn't tell me?"

"Oh wow. I didn't mention that either? We really need to catch up."

"No kidding." Lacy crossed her arms over her chest. "Give me the brief version."

"Liam knows a bit about bluegrass. We went there to see if we could find my uncle Chuck, and it worked. On the way back he asked me to trust him and let him take me into a cave. I stupidly agreed."

Lacy chuckled. "I like how you were so invested in telling me about your date with Liam that you blew past the fact that you found your great-uncle. You have to call and tell me all about everything later."

"If I survive the cave, I will. And it's not a date. At least, I don't think it is."

"Do you think he's going to try to kiss you?"

"No, I—"

"If he does try, you'll let him, right?"

"Lacy, this isn't a date," Hannah insisted. "He's helping me face my fears."

"Right. There's nothing romantic about the two of you alone in a dark, quiet cave—"

"Full of bats and spiders and who knows what else."

"With his strong arms to hold you if you get scared—"

"It's not like that." Hannah shook her head. "I have to get going. He's picking me up soon."

"Okay then. Call me later. I want to hear everything. Especially whether he's a good kisser."

"Goodbye, Lacy."

Hannah drove home, wondering if there was any chance Lacy was right. *Would* he try to kiss her? But that was ridiculous. It wasn't a date. He would have said if it was. She told herself not to be silly as she went up to her apartment and changed into jeans and a wool sweater. She put on hiking boots and headed downstairs.

Liam was sitting in his car, but he hopped out and opened her door before she reached the sidewalk. “Are you ready?” he asked, grinning.

“I guess so?”

He gave her a smile. “You’re going to be fine, I promise. You might even enjoy it.”

She tried to act confident as she climbed into the car and he closed the door, though inside she was trembling.

“So what did you think of Pastor Bob’s sermon this morning?” Liam asked as he drove toward the outskirts of town.

They talked about the sermon, and Liam shared that one of the hymns they’d sung, “Be Still My Soul,” was one of his favorites. “I sometimes sing it to myself as we’re driving to a fire,” Liam said. “Or any other time I feel afraid.”

“Wait. You’re afraid when you’re headed to a fire?”

“Every single time.”

“Really?” Hannah didn’t know why she’d never considered that. How could he do the job if he was afraid?

“Of course. I’m human, after all. I know what I do is dangerous. I’ve seen guys get hurt and have known people who didn’t make it. The danger is too real for me to ignore.”

“But you do it anyway. Why?”

“What do you mean?”

“Why would you do that to yourself? Why live in a constant state of terror?” It didn’t compute.

"To be clear, I said I get afraid, not that I live in a constant state of terror," Liam said. "There's a difference. But I do it because I truly love helping people. It's an adrenaline rush, for sure. But mostly, it's a chance to make a real difference in the world. It feels like what I'm meant to do."

"But if you're afraid every time..." She struggled to find the words to express what she was thinking. "Why do it? Why not get a job that doesn't make you afraid?"

"You mean, why don't I get a nice sedate desk job? Be an accountant or something?"

Hannah laughed at the idea of Liam in a suit and tie, carrying a briefcase to work. "Well, maybe not that, but—I don't know, something else?"

"Like open a business?" Liam asked. "Can you honestly tell me you weren't afraid when you opened your restaurant?"

"No," Hannah admitted. "Goodness. I'm afraid all the time. What if no one likes my food? What if a better restaurant opens in town? What if the business goes under, and I have to tell my staff they're all out of a job?"

"But you do it anyway," Liam pointed out.

"Yeah, but it's not like I'm going to die if I fail," Hannah said.

"It's a different kind of fear," Liam said. "You face it every day and do your best to overcome it so you can keep going. And that's what being brave is, right? It's not the absence of fear but doing things even in the face of it."

Hannah mulled that over. "I guess you're right."

"Of course I am."

She laughed. "Oh yeah?"

"I mean I'm not always, but when it comes to this stuff, I know a thing or two about it. I'm Liam the Brave, remember?"

Hannah grinned. "Well, if you catch me singing 'Be Still My Soul' in that cave, you'll know why."

"There's nothing scary about this cave. You're going to love it. And it's right up here." Liam pulled onto a country road that eventually led to a rutted dirt road. Finally, he parked under a grove of trees, and she was glad to see there were a few other cars there. At least they wouldn't be alone down there if something went wrong.

Liam opened her door then led her to the trunk. He pulled out a backpack and two hard hats with headlamps attached. "I think this should fit you, but try it on and see."

He helped her fit the helmet on snugly, and then he slung the backpack over his shoulder and started down a narrow path. "It's over that way," he said.

She followed him to what looked like a giant hole in the ground, but when they got closer, Hannah could see that it was a depression that was open on one side, overhung with rock. It was the entrance to the cave—at least twenty feet wide and probably fifteen feet high.

"Okay, this is a much less intimidating opening than the one on Lacy's farm," Hannah said. That cave entrance was little more than a hole in the ground, while this one looked like an actual cave.

"I told you."

They descended the grassy slope toward the opening, and Liam switched on his headlamp. Hannah did the same and followed him into a large open cavern. There was a steep slope down one side, but the other side was relatively level, and he walked along this ridge as they moved away from the bright light of the opening and into the dark of the cave.

She could handle this.

"It narrows up here," Liam said, pointing to a place where the walls seemed to have been pinched together.

They had to crouch to get through the narrow gap, but not for long. There was more room when they emerged into another open cavern on the other side. The ceiling was lower, and the daylight was gone, but the light from their headlamps was enough to see by. Stalactites hung from the ceiling, and stalagmites rose up to meet them. Higher up on the walls, the water had carved the rock into rounded bands of stone. From somewhere deep inside the cave, there was the sound of running water. It was unearthly, strange, and undeniably beautiful.

"Not too bad, right?"

"It's really wonderful."

"Wait until you see the next section."

She followed him through the cavern to what looked like a solid wall of rock.

"Okay, here's where it gets a little tricky," Liam said. He pointed to the base of the wall, and she saw that the stone didn't go all the way to the ground. There was an opening that was maybe eighteen inches high. "We're going to have to slide under that."

"Seriously?" Hannah felt her pulse speed up and her throat begin to close as she stared at the narrow opening. It was long enough, width-wide, for her body to slide through, but so shallow she wasn't sure she could fit through it, let alone get back out. "I don't know about this." What was on the other side? What if they couldn't come out again?

"I know it looks small, but you can do this. Once you get through, it's totally worth it."

She still hesitated.

"If you can get through it—and you can—you will get back out," Liam said, his voice calm. He put his hand on her arm. "So you don't need to worry about that. And I'll help you. You'll be safe."

She believed him in her head, but her whole body screamed for her to get out of there. She did not want to crawl through that hole into a place where she could get trapped. She reminded herself that being brave was not the absence of fear but acting in spite of the fear. The way she and Liam did every day in their jobs.

"Okay?" Liam asked gently.

"Okay," Hannah said, and she hoped she sounded more sure than she felt.

Liam took off his backpack and slid it through the opening. "I'll go first," he said. "And I'll be waiting on the other side."

Hannah had to fight not to beg him to stay, but he slid quickly and easily under the hanging rock and through the opening, disappearing to the other side. Now that she was left alone, she didn't want to go forward, but she certainly didn't want to go back. She thought of one of the verses of Liam's favorite hymn.

Be still my soul, thy God doth undertake
To guide the future as He has the past.
Thy hope, thy confidence let nothing shake;
All now mysterious shall be bright at last.

She knelt on the ground and took a deep breath.

"Just get on your stomach and slide right through." Liam's voice was muffled from the other side of the rock.

She lay down and felt the cold of the stone floor through her pants.

Be still my soul thy best, thy heavenly friend,
Through thorny ways leads to a joyful end.

She began to slide under the hanging rock and pushed her way through until she was on the other side of the wall.

"You did it!" Liam grinned at her. He reached out an arm and pulled her to her feet. "I knew you could."

Hannah took a second to make sure she was steady on her feet, and then she looked around at the room they were in. "Oh wow."

The rock above them resembled the arched ceiling of a church or a museum, but it was natural, made entirely of stone. Around the room, different formations of rocks, produced by many years of water running through the cavern, created bizarre and beautiful shapes in the shadows. Below them, down a steep slope, was a small creek. The room was enormous and breathtaking. She pulled out her phone and took pictures, trying and failing to capture the ethereal beauty of the place.

"This is amazing. And it's been here, under the ground, this whole time?" How had she never known about this?

"It sure has. Isn't it beautiful?"

Hannah spun around in a circle, casting the beam of light from her headlamp over the corners of the room. Everywhere she turned, there was a stunning formation of rock. It was like nothing she'd ever seen. "Who knew this was down here, underneath the cornfields?"

"There are places like this under cornfields all over Kentucky," Liam said. "Just waiting to be discovered."

"I see what you mean, about appreciating God's creation," Hannah said.

Liam smiled knowingly. And perhaps it was wishful thinking, but she thought she saw a particular kind of warmth in his eyes. Or maybe it was simply the light from the headlamps.

They stood in the dark room, taking it all in for a few more minutes, until they began to hear voices approaching from farther inside the cave.

"We could keep going if you want, but it gets pretty narrow up ahead," Liam said. "Then there's a big descent, so I don't know how much you would enjoy it. This was the part I wanted you to see."

"You promised me no scary descents, so I'll pass," Hannah said.

He grinned and gestured to the opening. "Why don't you go through it first? I'll follow right behind you."

This time she slid through with little hesitation, and soon she was back in the room with the stalactites and stalagmites. It was still beautiful and otherworldly and amazing, and she couldn't believe she'd almost let her fear get the best of her. She would have missed all of it.

"Thank you for bringing me here," she said after Liam slid his backpack and then himself through the opening. "I'm glad I got to see this."

"I'm glad you got to see it too. I'm proud of you for taking the chance, even though you weren't sure about it." He pushed himself to his feet and slung the backpack over his shoulders. "See? It's not so scary."

Hannah didn't exactly agree. "Actually, it was terrifying. But I was able to do it because I knew I could trust you."

Seeing the smile on his face made every scary moment worth it.

Chapter Nineteen

A part of Hannah hoped that Liam might ask her to dinner after they made it out of the cave, but he had to report to the station that evening, so he took her home and gave her a quick hug when he dropped her off. A friendly hug. Or was it more than that? She went up the stairs replaying moments from the day in her mind. She hadn't known what to expect that morning, but she knew this was a day she would not forget anytime soon.

She walked inside her apartment, sat down on the couch, and started scrolling through the photos she'd taken. They didn't capture the incredible strangeness and beauty of being in that cavern. Not even close. As she had experienced, a person couldn't really understand it unless they went there.

Which, she supposed, was kind of the point. That was no doubt why Liam, Ryder, Colt, Uncle Chuck, and so many others like them went exploring in caves in the first place. Being inside one was like nothing she'd ever experienced.

She chose a couple of the best photos and texted them to Lacy. I MADE IT OUT ALIVE, she wrote beneath the photos.

I KNEW YOU WOULD, Lacy wrote back. DID HE TRY TO KISS YOU?

IT WASN'T LIKE THAT. WE'RE JUST FRIENDS.

Lacy sent a sad face emoji.

Hannah laughed and was about to put her phone down, but then she decided to text some photos to Ryder to show him she'd braved it.

Today I went inside a cave and didn't die, she texted, and sent the same photos to him.

You've got it bad, was all he wrote back.

What did that mean? She texted a series of question marks.

I know how much you dislike caves. Which means you must like Liam a whole lot to agree to go into one.

We're just friends!

Ryder responded with a wink emoji.

Hannah gave up and decided to go wash off the cave dust.

She'd barely gotten out of the shower and was contemplating what to make for dinner when her phone rang.

She answered immediately. "Hi, Nana."

"Hello, dear," Nana said. "I talked with Roger today."

"How did he respond to the news?" Hannah asked.

"Better than I would have thought," she said. "I showed him the article in that magazine and pointed out the picture of him as a baby in the background. I said I was sure it was Chuck, and he agreed it must be. And he said he wants to meet him."

"That's understandable, and also very brave."

"I thought so too. Naturally, he's curious. Why wouldn't he be?"

"He probably wants some answers too, I would imagine," Hannah said.

"He's not the only one," Nana replied. "I've spent most of my life mourning my brother. Now I find out he was alive the whole time.

You better believe I'm going to demand some answers as soon as I'm done hugging him."

"Well, it might take some time to track down contact information for him, but now that we know what name he's using, it shouldn't be that hard. I'm sure we could use the info for the band if we can't find anything more concrete."

"I suppose you could do it that way, but we had another idea."

"What's that?"

"Roger checked out the band's website, and he saw that they have a show this week."

"Really?" She opened her laptop and found the band's website again. Then she clicked on their list of upcoming gigs. "You're right. There's a concert in Louisville tomorrow night."

"I think Roger wants to go to that."

"And do what?" Hannah wasn't sure that was such a good idea. "It's one thing if he merely wants to see him and listen to the music. But if he's thinking of confronting him—"

"Oh, no," Nana said. "I don't imagine he'd want to do that."

"And what about you?" Hannah asked. "Do you just want to see him?"

There was a moment of silence, and then Nana said, "I don't know. The honest truth is that I'm not sure I want to see him at all. I've spent so long believing he's gone, and it would almost be easier to continue believing it. When we thought he died, it devastated my mother. She was never the same afterward. It was a really dark time, and thinking about seeing him again brings it all back up for me." She paused before continuing. "So of course I want to know the truth. But I'm not totally sure I'm ready to see him again just yet.

I think I may need some time to wrap my head around this and pray about it."

"That makes sense," Hannah said. It sounded like Nana wouldn't go racing off to Louisville tomorrow night after all.

"But I think Roger does want to go. You should talk to him. Maybe you two should attend together."

It was Hannah's turn to hesitate. "Do you think that's a good idea? Driving all that way to see him when we don't plan to speak to him? Doesn't it make more sense just to find his contact information and reach out that way?"

"I don't know. You should talk to Roger. It sounds like he really wants to go, and I got the sense he won't be talked out of it. If he does decide to do this crazy thing, I'd rather someone goes with him. Someone who understands what's going on and has a level head on her shoulders."

Recalling how panicked she'd been about a small space in a rock wall a few short hours before, Hannah wasn't sure she agreed with her grandmother's assessment. But what else could she say? "Okay, Nana. I'll give him a call."

"Let me know what you all decide."

"I will," Hannah said. "And thank you."

"No, thank *you*, Hannah."

They hung up, and Hannah called Roger right away.

"I can't believe you found him, Hannah," was the first thing he said when he picked up.

"I'm just grateful we're not too late," Hannah said. "I bet I can track down contact information for him, but Nana said you were thinking of going to the concert in Louisville tomorrow night."

"I'm going, for sure," Roger said. "Now that I know he's out there, I have to. He's in his eighties. I need to talk to him before it's too late."

"I get that," Hannah said. "But he must be pretty healthy if he's still performing. Maybe it makes sense to wait and think this through, or try to reach out to him first. You could send an email or write a letter."

Part of Hannah hated that she was urging caution. She wanted to see Chuck as much as Roger did—well, okay, maybe not quite as much as Roger did, but a lot. But she was also worried about what might happen if their first interaction was a public confrontation. If all the pain and disappointment of learning his father walked away from him as a baby came out when Roger saw him.

And how would Chuck respond? He'd disappeared on purpose and started a new life. He wanted them to think he was dead. He might have a family now, and a whole world that would be upset by the reappearance of his son. It might go horribly wrong. In fact, Hannah couldn't think of any other possibility. It wasn't as if a conversation would take back the last sixty years.

"I know you're right, of course," Roger said. "In pretty much every way, it would be smarter to wait and contact him first. But I can't make myself wait on this, Hannah. Now that I know he's out there, I need to see him. I need to meet him for myself. I'm planning to go to that concert tomorrow night. You can come with me or not, but either way, I'm going."

Hannah realized it was out of her hands. She'd done the work of tracking Chuck down, but it was no longer her situation to manage. It wasn't up to her what Roger did with the information now that he had it. She'd given her advice, but ultimately it was his choice.

This was, and always had been, way bigger than her desire to solve a mystery. It was Roger's life, and it had changed radically. Everything he thought he'd known about his family had been turned upside down. She was in no place to try to stop him from meeting his father. She could only decide whether she wanted to be with him when he did.

She took a deep breath. "I'll be there,"

Hannah received a text while she got ready for bed. She set her toothbrush down, rinsed out her mouth, and picked up her phone. It was from Liam. I HAD A GREAT TIME TODAY. YOU DID AN AMAZING JOB.

Hannah typed out a response and then deleted it and started over and then deleted that one again. She tried to find the right mix of funny and flirty, but not too flirty, yet also sincere. Finally, after several attempts, she realized she was overthinking it and just wrote THANK YOU FOR TAKING ME TODAY. I HAD A GREAT TIME TOO, AND I DON'T HATE CAVES QUITE AS MUCH AS I USED TO.

She waited a few minutes to see if he would respond, but he didn't. She decided to stop obsessing and get some sleep. She shut off the ringer on her phone and climbed into bed, still replaying scenes from the cave excursion in her mind. She'd actually done it. She'd faced her fears with Liam. And even kind of enjoyed it.

She was remembering the feel of his hand on her arm as she drifted off to sleep.

Chapter Twenty

Hannah slept in on Monday. She ate a leisurely breakfast and read her devotional, and then she went downstairs to the restaurant. Even though it was her day off, there was plenty to do, and she planned to spend the day catching up on emails and invoices.

But she needed more coffee first, so she headed down to Jump Start. There were a few people in line, and the coffee shop was buzzing. She wasn't surprised to find Dylan there, hunched over his laptop again. The SAT study guide was open in front of him.

"Hey, Hannah." He slipped his headphones off his ears. "Guess what?"

"What?"

"I downloaded the application for Western Kentucky University. I'm really going to do it."

"That's amazing. Congratulations, Dylan."

"I might not get in."

"But you might. And you'll never know unless you try. I'm proud of you for taking this step."

His ears flushed pink. "Thank you for encouraging me."

"You're awesome, Dylan. I know you can do this."

"Thanks." He was smiling as he went back to his computer.

Hannah got in line, thinking about what bravery really meant. Sometimes it didn't mean rushing into burning buildings. Sometimes it meant facing fears head-on. Sometimes it meant making the first move, even when she wished someone else would do it. Sometimes it meant confronting the truth when it would be easier to hold on to a long-standing lie. And sometimes it meant taking a chance on a heart's desire despite the very real risk of failure. She couldn't be prouder of Dylan. She felt the same way about Raquel, asking Marshall out the other night. And Roger, for planning to face his long-lost father.

And she even felt that way about herself for facing her fear of caves.

After she got her coffee, Hannah spent most of the day processing invoices for the restaurant and then taking care of personal chores and errands. Then she ate a quick dinner and got ready to go to Louisville, putting on a cute denim skirt and boots. She even bothered to curl her hair.

When she was ready, she drove over to Dad and Uncle Gabriel's house. Roger was meeting them at the concert venue. When Dad found out about the plan to drive to Louisville, he insisted on coming along. Hannah wasn't sure whether he truly wanted to meet his uncle so badly or whether he just wanted to be there for her. But either way she was glad to have him on the long drive. Uncle Gabriel had wanted to come too, but he had plans to eat dinner with Maeve and her family. Hannah and Dad promised to fill him in on what happened.

"I've been listening to this band's music," Dad said, climbing into the passenger seat and closing the door. "They're really good."

"That's what all the articles say," Hannah said.

He buckled his seat belt. "Doesn't mean I like it. But I did enjoy this. The way they play all those strings all at once is incredible. And the sound takes you back to another time."

Hannah agreed that bluegrass music was nostalgic, and that was no doubt part of its appeal. But it also contained many layers and so much depth, much more than seemed possible from a few stringed instruments. She'd heard bluegrass in the background for much of her life—growing up in Kentucky, it was hard not to—but she had actually listened to it for the first time and understood how a certain kind of sound could evoke a feeling and a history of a place and its people. Bluegrass, for better or for worse, felt like home.

"Boneyard Blues it is." Hannah plugged in her phone and found a playlist of songs from the band. She started the music before she pulled away from the curb. The show was supposed to start at seven, and Louisville was a ninety-minute drive. They had allowed two hours to make sure they had enough time to find parking and buy tickets.

While she drove, Dad talked about an educational TV show he and Uncle Gordon enjoyed watching together and about a trick he was trying to teach Zeus. "It's definitely taking him longer than usual to pick up, but it's a pretty advanced trick. He'll get it sooner or later," he said with his usual calm. "How are things at the restaurant?"

"It's going well," Hannah said. "We're busy most nights, which is great. Of course, things are usually slower in the winter months at restaurants, so I'm already thinking about incentives to get people to come in. But for now we're operating at a level I'm comfortable with, which is a huge blessing."

"It seems like you're always at work. I worry about you working too hard."

She sent him a quick smile. Her father always fussed over her. "You can't own a restaurant without working hard. But it's what I signed up for. It's what I love."

"I just don't want you spending all your time at work. You're young. You should be enjoying your life."

What he meant—as usual—was that she should be dating someone, but he knew better than to say so out loud, since she'd set boundaries around that particular conversation. Initially, he'd been a bit overbearing about it, but he'd backed off when Hannah expressed discomfort.

"I am enjoying it, Dad," she assured him. "I'm literally living my dream. Owning my own restaurant is what I've always wanted. These first few years are going to be extra-hard work, but it'll get easier, as long as we're able to keep attracting customers."

"Gordon and I will continue to do our best to eat enough to keep you in business, in that case," he said with a grin. Then he added more seriously, "I worry about you. That's all."

"I know you do. But I'm doing okay. Really."

"I want more than just okay for you, but if you're content right now, I'll try to let it go. I'm a dad. I can't help wanting you to be wildly happy rather than simply getting by."

Hannah knew parents always worried about their children, even though she didn't have children of her own. But since Mom's death, she'd heard Dad say it out loud more. With Mom gone, he seemed to feel the need to hold on to his remaining family even tighter.

"Thanks, Dad. I love you too," she said. He hadn't said those specific words to her, but she was well aware that they were behind the sentiment he'd expressed.

They listened to the Boneyard Blues music for most of the drive, and when they got to Louisville and found the venue—a converted warehouse in a gentrifying industrial neighborhood—he helped her find parking. She was able to parallel park with only a little back and forth, which felt like a victory. They made their way to the door, paid for their tickets, and found Roger already inside, sipping a soda from the bar in the front room. He wore fitted jeans and a checked flannel shirt with boots, and Hannah was surprised to see how stylish he was. He must be eager to make a good impression on his father if they spoke.

"You made it," he said. "This place is something, isn't it?"

Hannah looked around at the high ceilings and brick walls and had to agree. It was huge and had been nicely converted. But there was something missing. "Where's the stage?"

"Through there." Roger gestured to an opening in the wall down from the bar. "I peeked in earlier. It's a big space."

Dad went to the bar and got sodas for him and Hannah. When he returned, he asked Roger, "So, how are you feeling about all this?"

"I tried to figure that out the whole way here," Roger said. "And the truth is, I'm not sure. I'm excited. Nervous. Scared, if I'm honest. But mostly I'm ready for the truth. I want to know why he left us. Why he left me."

His voice cracked a bit on the last word. It was such a vulnerable thing to say that Hannah wasn't sure how to respond at first.

Thankfully, Dad jumped in. "Whatever his reasons, we know that he never stopped thinking about you. We know he kept your picture in his home all these years."

Roger shrugged. "It's not the same though, is it? Thinking about someone and actually being a part of their life are two different things."

"Of course they are," Dad said. "Hopefully soon we'll have a chance to hear his side of the story."

"Let's hope so."

People started moving away from the bar and into the main room, and the three of them joined the throng. There was a stage at the front and plenty of space to spread out, and they found a spot to stand in the middle of the crowd.

"I don't have much patience for a concert with no seats," Dad said, and Roger nodded his agreement.

Thankfully, soon enough the opening band came out and started playing. The opener was a young brother-and-sister duo, and they were very good, but Hannah couldn't help feeling impatient for the main event. After half a dozen songs and an encore, they announced that there would be a short break while the stage was reset, and the crowd began talking and moving around.

"They were pretty good," Hannah said, mostly to fill the time.

"They were very good," Roger agreed. "But I still wanted them to get off the stage so the headliner could come out already."

Hannah decided to use the break to get refills on their sodas, so she headed to the bar, along with about half the crowd. By the time she got back to the main room and threaded her way through the people, Boneyard Blues had been announced. Five men walked onto the stage, but Hannah really only saw one.

There he was. It was undeniably, obviously Chuck. His hair was white, and his posture was stooped, and he shuffled slowly to the spot where his fiddle case was, but it was him. He was clean-shaven now, and she could see the high cheekbones and the rounded chin from the photos when he was young. He wore jeans and a tan jacket over a black T-shirt and boots.

"That's the guy who came to my door," Roger said. "It was him all along."

The crowd roared as the musicians picked up their instruments and started tuning them. When the guitar player stepped to the microphone, the cheers only got louder. Chuck was busy tuning his fiddle and running rosin along his bow, but as soon as the first song started, he was right there, sawing out the notes of the song. It was a song that was on the playlist Hannah and her dad had listened to, and it was clear the crowd recognized it. Most people started dancing and singing along. It was a good song, about new love after a broken heart, and Hannah enjoyed it even more than she had earlier, because of the energy of the crowd and the excitement of hearing it live.

After the first song ended, the guitar player introduced each of the musicians, and the crowd cheered after each name. When he introduced Wayne Miller, the crowd roared.

"Legend!" a man near Hannah called out, and people around him clapped and hooted.

Hannah supposed Chuck was something of a legend in these circles. He was one of the two original members of this band, which had been performing for more than fifty years. That was undeniably incredible.

The band started the next song, and it was new to her, but she enjoyed it. It was about a little chapel in the woods and some of the miracles that had happened there. But even as she listened and nodded her head to the music, she was impatient. Impatient for the show to be over, for...she didn't know what, exactly. Now that they were there, she had no real idea if they would be able to approach Chuck or what they would say if they could. Would they be allowed anywhere near him? She hadn't realized quite how big a star he was in this world. Surely there was security keeping random people from wandering backstage. Was this whole trip a waste of time?

But she looked at Roger, saw the tears running down his cheeks in the dark concert hall, and she knew it wasn't a waste. Whatever else happened there, he'd seen his father in the flesh, knowing it was him. If nothing else happened, this was important.

After the band had played for more than an hour, they took a bow then came back for an encore. Hannah looked around, trying to figure out how to get backstage, how they would find a way to meet Chuck.

When the band took their final bow, the crowd cheered, and then the five men walked off the stage and through a door to the right. Members of the crowd started moving toward the exit, but Hannah was already making her way past the stage, followed by Dad and Roger. She approached the backstage door and was shocked to see there was no one guarding it, at least on this side. She glanced around to see if anyone would stop her then turned the knob. The door swung open, revealing a too-bright hallway lit with fluorescent lights. She stepped inside, her dad and Roger right behind her.

They'd only made it a few steps before a booming voice called out, "Can I help you?"

Hannah turned and saw a large man in a black suit walking toward them.

"We're looking for Chuck Lynch," Hannah said, holding her shoulders back as confidently as she could.

"We need to see your credentials," a second guard said, stepping up behind the first one.

"And we need to speak to Chuck Lynch," Roger replied.

The guards didn't seem to care about this information. Why would they? They had no idea who Chuck was. "You can't come back here," the first one said. "Not without the proper credentials."

"Chuck will want to see us," Dad said. "If you could just let him know we're here—"

"Unless you can show us credentials, I'm going to have to ask you to leave," said the second guard. Both guards were large men, and Hannah had no doubt they could eject the three of them easily enough.

But she had to try again. They'd come all this way. After everything they'd been through to get to this point, she wasn't about to give up.

"Could we please just check with Chuck? You know him as Wayne Miller. We're family. If he doesn't want to see us, we'll leave, but I have a feeling he'll let us in."

"If you can't show us your credentials, I'm going to need you to turn around right now and walk out of here." The first guard took a menacing step forward.

Hannah heard the words that had come out of his mouth. She understood what they meant. But she wasn't quite ready to do as he asked.

Instead, she kept walking down the hall, headed who knew where. All she knew was that she couldn't leave until she found Chuck. Until Roger could talk to his father face-to-face after all this time. She was going to be brave—and maybe, possibly, more than a little bit foolish—and find her great-uncle.

"Ma'am, you can't go back there." The first guard hustled in front of her and blocked her way.

Roger followed Hannah's lead and joined her.

"Stop right there!" The second guard pushed past Roger to add his bulk to their barrier.

Suddenly Hannah had visions of the three of them in the back of a police car, and she wondered if they really did need to listen before things got out of hand.

"We're here to see Chuck Lynch," Roger said loudly.

"You'll have to contact him another way, because you all need to get out of here now." The first guard walked forward, trying to force them to back up. Hannah was pretty sure he could pick her up and forcibly remove her if she didn't go willingly. She should obey, she knew she should.

But just before she gave up, she shouted, as loudly as she could, "Chuck Lynch, if you're in there, Roger is here to see you!"

There was no response. If Chuck was still here, he either hadn't heard or didn't care. The second thought was nearly paralyzing. Was it possible that Chuck had heard and wasn't going to come out? Or was the band already gone, headed home to sleep or on some tour bus, headed for their next show?

In any case, the guards forced them toward the door, and in a moment, it wouldn't matter, because they would be thrown out of there anyway—if they weren't arrested. The second guard had the stage door open when a voice sounded at the far end of the hallway.

"Stop." When the guards didn't respond quickly enough, the voice rose to a bellow. "I said *stop*!"

Everyone, including Hannah, froze and turned toward the sound of the voice. Chuck stood there. He had taken off the jacket and wore jeans and a T-shirt. His stance was wide, his hands were on his hips, and he looked ready to charge them all. Even in his eighties, he cut an intimidating figure. "Let those people alone."

"Mr. Miller, these visitors don't have credentials," the first guard said. "I'm afraid they can't come back here."

"Yes, they can," Chuck said.

"I'm afraid protocol dictates—"

"I don't care about your protocol," Chuck interrupted. "You're going to let them through immediately. That man doesn't need credentials to see me."

The first guard relaxed his stance. "He doesn't?"

Chuck took in a deep breath, and then let it out slowly. "No, he doesn't. He's my son."

Chapter Twenty-One

Before they knew what was happening, the guards had disappeared and Chuck was running toward them. He moved fast for someone in his eighties, and a moment later, he threw his arms around Roger and held him as they both sobbed.

"I've wanted to do this every day for the last sixty years," Chuck said as he pulled his son closer. "I never stopped thinking about you."

"Dad," was all Roger said, but that simple word was enough to bring tears to Hannah's eyes.

A few minutes later, they entered a dressing room in the back. They all cried—even Hannah's dad, who kept brushing away tears discreetly, as if he thought no one would notice.

When they were seated, Chuck looked around at them. "I know Roger, but I'm not sure who the two of you are."

Dad reached his hand out. "I'm Gabriel Prentiss. Your sister, Elsa's, younger son."

Chuck's hands flew to his mouth. "You're Gabriel?" Tears gathered in his eyes once again.

Dad nodded. "And this is my daughter, Hannah."

"It's wonderful to meet you." Hannah held out her hand, and he shook it, his eyes wide.

"You were a baby when I last saw you," Chuck said to Dad. "Just a tiny little thing. And now—look at you. You're all grown, with an adult daughter."

"A lot has happened since you've been gone," Dad said.

"How's Gordon?" Chuck asked.

"He's doing great. We're both retired, and we share a house," Dad said. "He wanted to be here tonight, but he's having dinner with his daughter and her family."

"That's amazing." Chuck shook his head. "And your mother?"

"She's still around and doing great. Dad too."

A fresh wave of tears welled up for Chuck. "I'm so glad."

"She was very surprised to hear that he's alive," Dad said.

"I guess that brings up the question." Chuck wiped the back of his arm across his eyes, grabbed a water bottle, and took a long drink. "How did you find me? I thought—well, I was sure everyone thought I was dead."

"We did think that," Dad said. "Everyone thought you died in a cave collapse."

Chuck nodded but didn't say anything.

Hannah took up the tale. "But then, a little over a week ago, my cousin Ryder—that's Uncle Gordon's son—was exploring in the caves under Bluegrass Hollow Farm. They found another way into the passage that got sealed off when you—" She was going to say *died*, but that obviously wasn't right. "When you disappeared. Inside, he found your things. Things that made it clear you didn't die like everyone thought."

"There was another way into that cavern?" Chuck asked.

"Apparently from above," Hannah confirmed. "Once they found your things and no signs of a body, it was clear that you hadn't died in the cave like everyone thought, and we started trying to track you down. To find out what really happened."

"What really happened," Chuck murmured, almost to himself. "I guess now that you're here, I should tell you that. It's a story I never thought I would have to tell."

"It would mean a lot to us all," Hannah said. "To hear the truth."

Chuck didn't say anything for a minute. He just looked at his son, his eyes full of sorrow.

"I think we deserve that, at the very least," Roger said.

Chuck took another sip from the water bottle, and Hannah saw that his hand shook. She didn't know whether that was from nerves or if he had a medical condition. But in that moment, as excited as she was, she was reminded that Chuck was over eighty years old, and his life had just changed completely. No matter how much they wanted—deserved—answers, he also deserved grace.

"Walking away from you and your mom was the hardest thing I've ever done in my life," Chuck said slowly. "I loved her. I loved you even more."

"Then why did you do it?" Roger asked. "How could you desert us like that?"

"I've asked myself that same question a thousand times over the years," Chuck said. "And the truth is, I wish I could go back and undo it. Erase all those years and do it over again. I don't think I would make the same decision today. I'm older and hopefully wiser now. Back then—and I would understand if you can't believe me, but this is the truth—I honestly thought you two would be better off without me. I knew I was ruining your mother's life, living the way I was. It wasn't fair to her. I was in debt. She worked so hard, and I was just messing it up."

He took another sip from the bottle before he went on. "We were too young when we got married. She was able to handle it, but I wasn't. I was immature and self-centered, and I made bad decisions that you and your mother had to pay for, again and again. I knew I was letting her down. I knew I was a terrible father. I knew how frustrated and angry and desperate I was making your mother. But I couldn't seem to stop. I wanted to be better, but I was weak. I gambled more than I could afford to lose. And I hated myself for it."

Hannah felt her anger at this man begin to melt into compassion. She'd heard that gambling, like other addictions, was an illness rather than a conscious choice. That was exactly what Chuck was describing.

"One night, as I was walking home after losing the month's rent on the horses—again—I started thinking more seriously about how the two of you would be better off without me. That if I disappeared, it would be better for everyone. That I should walk away and give your mother a fresh start. The idea wouldn't go away, and I realized that simply leaving wasn't good enough. She wouldn't be able to start fresh without me if I just left. She needed to think I was gone for good. She needed to think I'd died, and then she would be free."

"Couldn't you have filed for divorce?" Hannah asked. "Then she would have been free rather than grieving your loss. Wouldn't that have been easier?"

"In some ways, maybe, but I knew Minnie would never go for it. She would continue to demand that I do better. And I wanted to, but no matter what I did, I couldn't. The church would never grant us an annulment, because there was nothing invalid about the marriage, and divorce had a harsher stigma than it does now. I couldn't put her through that."

Hannah knew no one went into a marriage expecting to get divorced. It was always a decision mired in heartbreak. But she still didn't see why it wouldn't have been better than the option Chuck had chosen. "Okay, then what about separating?"

"I know this doesn't make sense, but I loved Minnie too much for that," Chuck said. "I knew she needed to be able to find someone better and my son needed a better father figure in his life. As long as we were officially married, Minnie would never allow herself to find that person."

"Did you think of trying to become that person yourself?" Roger asked.

"I tried so many times." Chuck shook his head. "I wanted to, Son. I really did. But I always made the wrong decision. I always thought I was one race away from winning big. Good luck was right around the corner. I was going to make it up to your mom as soon as I got it all back. But I never did, and it was terrible to see myself let her down, over and over. I was tired of failing. I guess that's the truth. I was tired of disappointing everyone, including myself."

Hannah wanted to argue that he could have tried harder. Of course, she'd never faced an addiction, so the situation was far more complicated than she could imagine. Plus, it wasn't her place to speak up. She had no right to judge him or his choices. All she could do was listen.

"So I started planning. You have to understand, back then, I thought it was the most selfless thing I could do. If I died, you and your mom would be free, and you could start a new life. I thought it was the best outcome for everyone. The only person who would suffer for my bad decisions was me."

It made a sad kind of sense. It was as Harold had suspected—Chuck truly had believed he was doing what was best for his family. His logic may have been warped, but his intentions weren't.

"Why did you decide to make it look like you'd died in a cave?" Roger asked. "Of all the terrible ways you could have done it, that's one of the worst ones I can think of."

"I didn't want to just disappear," Chuck said. "I knew that would lead to a search. I needed everyone to think there was no way I could have survived. Some way for me to die, but where it wouldn't seem odd that there was no body, you know? That section of cave was always on the verge of collapse anyway. It was perfect. I went in and left my things behind, everything I thought might point to what I was planning to do or tie me to my old life, and then I knocked the rocks down on my way out. As they fell, I knew no one was getting back into that section of cave anytime soon. It would be a death wish to try."

"But they did try," Dad said. "Rescuers spent days putting their own lives in danger trying to get to you."

Chuck shook his head. "I'm sorry about that. I truly am. I didn't know they would do that."

"You didn't think they would try to get you out?" Hannah said.

"I didn't think anyone would care enough," Chuck said. "I promise. I thought they would see the car, discover the fallen rock, and assume I was a goner. It never occurred to me that people would put their own lives in danger for mine."

"Why wouldn't they?" Roger asked.

"Because I wasn't worth it. That's how I honestly felt. I thought they'd all thank the Lord there was one less problem in their lives and move on."

Hannah could see that he really believed that, and it broke her heart. He truly believed no one would think his life worth saving. It said so much about his sense of self-worth at the time and shed light on why he believed his family might be better off without him. It was as tragic as it was wrong. People had loved him, enough to try to save him at great personal cost.

"What if you'd gotten trapped in that tunnel when you knocked the rock down?" Dad asked. "Did you ever think about that possibility?"

"I did," Chuck said. "And I decided it was worth the risk. If I truly had died—well, that wouldn't have been the worst thing in the world."

Hannah hated hearing how little he'd thought his life was worth. Hearing the story from him, she felt for him and his younger self—lost and feeling utterly alone.

"But you did make it out," Roger said.

"We found a receipt for a bus ticket in the cave," Hannah said. "So I assume you took a bus to start your new life. But how did you get to Bowling Green?"

"I hitchhiked," he said. "I hid until a car came along that I didn't recognize, and when I saw that it wasn't anyone from town, I stuck out my thumb. It wasn't so unusual in those days. I was lucky to be picked up by a guy who was just passing through. I imagine he never heard about a fellow trapped in a cave nearby."

"You changed your clothes before you left the cave," Hannah said.

"Everyone in town saw me in that shirt," Chuck said. "I needed to be wearing something no one would recognize, in case I was seen. I put on sunglasses and a hat, and it worked."

"We also found a receipt from a pawn shop in your wallet," Hannah said. "You sold a ring, a watch, and cuff links before you left."

"I hated to do it," Chuck said. "Those cuff links were a wedding present. The watch was my grandfather's. But I needed bus fare and some cash to get me started in Louisville. At the time, it seemed like the only way. Now I wish I'd done things differently. I wish I'd done so many things differently."

It was quiet for a moment in the wake of his words. Hannah believed him. It was clear how much his past decisions pained him.

"So, you changed your clothes, climbed out of the cave, hitchhiked to the bus station in Bowling Green, and then you went where?" Dad asked.

"We found a map in the cave," Hannah said. "Three cities were marked—Nashville, Louisville, and Lexington."

"I went back and forth between the three of them," Chuck said. "But I settled on Louisville because it had the most jobs at the time. I thought I would get a job in a factory or something."

"But you took your fiddle," Hannah said. "You weren't planning on becoming a musician at that point?"

"I took the fiddle because I knew music would always be a part of my life," Chuck said. "But I had no intention of becoming a musician. That just happened because I needed a way to pay the bills. What I made in the factory didn't pay enough, so I started filling in for musicians here and there, and soon I was making more money playing music than I was doing line work. And then a buddy asked me to start a band with him, and—well, here we are." He shrugged. "I lived in fear that someone would recognize me once the band started taking off. But no one did."

"We all thought you were dead, so we weren't looking," Roger said. "Dead men don't play bluegrass."

"No, I suppose they don't," Chuck said. "That's why I got away with it."

"And obviously you changed your name," Dad said. "How did you get new documentation for that?"

"If you know the right people, that's not hard. Or at least, it wasn't at the time."

Liam had said the same thing. For the right price, probably anything could be done.

"So, that was it? You changed your clothes and your name, left behind your ID and everything that tied you to your life, and walked out of that cave? You never looked back?" The pain Roger felt was evident in his words and his tone. He was still trying to process everything, and the pain of discovering his father had chosen to walk away was probably overwhelming.

"Now that's where you're wrong," Chuck said. "I mean, the first part, yes. That's all true, sadly. I can't change it. I knew Chuck Lynch would be declared dead, and he was dead to me as well. I found a guy who could get me a new ID, and that was that. Chuck was gone."

Roger lowered his head, his jaw clenched.

"But the last part, about never looking back?" Chuck continued. "You're wrong there. Not a day went by when I didn't think about you.

Most of my life wasn't that hard to leave behind. I had no real career, no prospects. I was constantly faced with my own poor choices."

Roger raised his head and met his father's gaze.

"But leaving you? That nearly killed me. I missed you every single day, so much that it felt like a physical ache. I thought about coming back to see you so many times. But I couldn't, because I knew you had a better life with your mom than I could ever give you. I checked on you both when I could. I would pay attention to the news in Blackberry Valley, and then in Bowling Green when you all moved there. I went to the library and read the archives in the paper every few years. I read about your mother getting remarried. Your stepfather seemed like a good man."

"You knew she was married? While you were still alive?" Roger asked. "You didn't think to warn her that she was committing bigamy?"

"Chuck was dead, remember? Not just in her mind, but in my own as well. I didn't see it as bigamy, because Chuck was gone in every way that mattered. And I was glad for her. I was glad for you. That was what I wanted, when I left—a better life for you both."

"Uncle Don was a good man," Dad told Chuck. "He made Minnie happy."

"He was good to me," Roger added. "He was a great dad. But he wasn't you. It was one thing to believe you died. It's another thing entirely to know that you've been alive the whole time and just walked away."

"I know you may never understand," Chuck said. "And that's something I have to live with. But I hope you can someday believe me that I did it because I truly thought it was the best thing for you."

Hannah didn't know if Chuck believed that or if he had to keep saying it to convince himself.

Roger pressed his lips together and looked down at his lap.

"I saw the announcement when you got married, and when your kids were born. Part of me still can't believe I'm a grandpa. And I saw when your mom passed. That was a sad day."

Roger's head snapped up again. "What do you care?" he asked, his tone harsh.

"I always loved your mother," Chuck said. There was no malice, no defensiveness in his voice, as if he felt he deserved Roger's anger. "I know you may not believe it, but I never stopped loving her."

"You had a funny way of showing it."

Chuck didn't flinch or argue with Roger. He merely looked at him, wonder in his eyes, like he still couldn't believe his son was there.

"What about you?" Hannah's dad asked. "Did you remarry?"

"No," Chuck said. "No other kids either. I had a few relationships over the years, but I never loved any of them like I loved Minnie, so they never lasted."

Roger was quiet, no doubt processing this.

"If you know all of this about us, why didn't you ever do anything about it?" Roger asked. "Did you ever think about coming out of hiding and making it right?"

"How would my coming back have made anything right?" Chuck asked gently. "Should I have reappeared and ruined your mother's happy marriage? I couldn't do that to her. I couldn't do that to you. And I was afraid you'd be angry. Not that you don't have every right to be. But I thought it was for the best. I don't know what else to say, except that I was trying to make things better for you. I left because I wanted your life to be better than the one I could give you, and I stayed away once I saw it was working."

Hannah didn't know what to say or do to cut the tension in the room. Roger was hurt. He was angry. And also, as she'd suspected, he was completely overwhelmed. Everything he understood about his life had been turned on its head. It would take some getting used to. Anyone would be thrown for a loop. She prayed that God would bring healing where there was hurt, and peace where there was anger. She prayed that the Lord would bless them both—bless them all—as they wrestled with how to move forward.

"It was you who stopped by my house asking for directions, wasn't it?" Roger said. "Fifteen years ago."

"That was me," Chuck said. "I had to drive through Bowling Green, and I knew you lived there. It wasn't hard to find your address, and I wanted to see you. I knew you were doing well from my research, but I had to see for myself."

"You could have told me who you were then," Roger said.

"What would you have done if I had?" Chuck cocked his head.

Roger didn't answer for a moment, and then he let out a chuckle. "I probably would have had a heart attack, to be honest."

"See? I would have gone and killed you before I even got a chance to get to know you."

Roger didn't exactly smile, but something in his face changed. He was still upset, for sure. There was a lot of anger to be worked through and healing that would need to happen. But that hint of a smile made Hannah hope it would. That out of the depths of his pain, healing would happen. And with time, the two of them would come to see eye to eye and begin to build a relationship.

"I'm so sorry," Chuck said. "I wish I could go back and do it all over again. But I can't, and all I can do is ask you to forgive me."

"I don't know that I can," Roger said. "Not right now, anyway. Not today. But I'll pray about it. I know God will help me get there."

It was a start. And maybe that was all anyone could hope for in the moment.

Hannah didn't know what the future would look like. She was pretty sure Chuck had broken more than a few laws in the process of starting a new life, and she didn't know if there would be ramifications for that all these years later. She knew there were many people he needed to apologize to. People he had hurt. When he vanished, he'd left a lot of pain in his wake.

But she also knew that with God, all things were possible. What was shattered could be made whole. Lies could be replaced by the truth. Fears could be overcome. Hearts healed. The truth had come to light, and that was a good place to start.

She didn't know what the days ahead would hold for these two. Or for others—because of course, Chuck's actions affected so many more people than were in this room. For so many people, this changed everything.

But sitting there, watching Roger and the father he'd thought was lost forever, she knew that nothing was impossible. And no matter what, God was in control.

She could see the love that this father had for his son, and how, buried beneath all that pain, Roger wanted to get to know his father. She had a feeling things would turn out just fine.

As they often did when one was brave and trusted in God's plan.

From the Author

Dear Reader,

When I started researching Barren County, in the western part of Kentucky where this story takes place, I discovered that Mammoth Cave National Park is right in this area and open to the public for tours. There are several other smaller but still spectacular underground caverns as well, such as Diamond Caverns, Onyx Cave, and Hidden River Cave. Not only that, but there are lots of noncommercialized caverns, like the fictional McLeod Cave in this story, all over the area. I started looking at pictures from inside these caves, and I was hooked.

I mean, not in the sense that I wanted to go *in* them. I'm like Hannah in that I get claustrophobic simply thinking about that. But these underground caverns are amazing and beautiful, and they are just creepy enough to make for a great setting for this story. So I created a mystery about someone living my worst nightmare—getting trapped in an underground cave—and had fun imagining what really happened when Chuck disappeared.

In researching this book, while I was trying to figure out what Ryder and Colt would have seen and experienced as they explored underground caverns, I found a number of informative and highly entertaining videos made by people who explore caves and post footage online. I will never understand what motivates these people, but

I'm glad they exist and that God made all of us different and unique. Those videos were invaluable as I tried to make this story realistic.

I also knew I wanted to bring bluegrass music into this story. I don't know a lot about it, but there are several bluegrass musicians at my church, and they have played during services and at fund-raisers to help restore our building. As I worked on this book, I was able to attend a concert put on by one of the musicians—to raise money to restore our historic but decrepit stained-glass windows—and I was reminded of what a beautiful, haunting genre it is. The lyrics, the style, and the sound itself are all so evocative of a specific place, and many of the songs are laced with faith. I was grateful to be able to learn more about bluegrass music as I wrote this book.

I'm loving this series, and I'm grateful to have been able to write this book for it. I hope you enjoyed reading it as much as I enjoyed writing it.

Best wishes,
Beth Adams

About the Author

Beth Adams lives in Brooklyn, New York, with her husband and two daughters. When she's not writing, she's trying to find time to read mysteries.

The Hot Spotlight

Mammoth Cave National Park

One of sixty-three national parks in the country, Mammoth Cave National Park near Cave City, Kentucky, covers over 52,000 acres and contains the largest known cave system in the world. With over 426 miles of underground passageways surveyed, it is nearly twice as large as the second-largest cave system, Mexico's Sac Actun. The national park was established in 1941, and was named a UNESCO World Heritage site in 1981.

People have lived in, explored, extracted minerals from, and used the system of caves for thousands of years. Artifacts have been found in Mammoth Cave from at least 1200 BC, and there is evidence of occupation by various tribes native to the Americas over thousands of years. Portions of the caves have been used as a mine for saltpeter, an ingredient in gunpowder, though tourism has been the main industry at the caverns for more than 200 years.

If you do go to visit the park, there are numerous ranger-led tours that will show off the highlights of these amazing caverns. Many of the most popular tours will take you deep into the earth, as you descend staircases through narrow passageways and well-marked and lighted tunnels. You'll pass deep pits, impressive rock formations, enormous domed areas, ornate flowstone, and the cavern's most famous formation, Frozen Niagara.

The well-lit and accessible areas covered by tours are nothing like the dangerous, unexplored caves showcased in this book, but they all speak of the creativity and power of the God who made them all.

From the Hot Spot Kitchen

JACOB'S FAMOUS PUMPKIN CHEESECAKE

Ingredients for crust:

2 graham crackers, crushed

⅓ cup sugar

½ cup melted butter

Directions:

Mix graham cracker crumbs, sugar, and melted butter and press into 9-inch springform or pie pan.

Ingredients for cheesecake filling:

24 ounces cream cheese, softened

¾ cup brown sugar

½ cup granulated sugar

⅓ cup sour cream

1½ teaspoons vanilla extract

1 cup pumpkin puree

2 teaspoons pumpkin spice

½ teaspoon cinnamon

3 large eggs, beaten

Directions:

Preheat oven to 350 degrees.

Beat cream cheese and sugars together in stand mixer. Add sour cream and mix well. Add vanilla extract, puree, and spices. Mix well. Add eggs, one at a time, until just mixed after each addition. Spread batter evenly over crust. Bake on center rack of oven until center is almost set, about 40 minutes. Allow to cool, and refrigerate overnight. Serve with whipped cream or, for more deliciousness, cinnamon or vanilla ice cream!

Read on for a sneak peek of another exciting book in the *Mysteries of Blackberry Valley* series!

Run for the Roses

BY CATE NOLAN

Sunlight dappled the back roads of Blackberry Valley, Kentucky, as a gentle breeze wafted through the trees and danced in the colorful leaves on overhanging branches. Endless pastures of rippling grasses spread out beneath a clear blue sky, not a cloud in sight on the glorious November morning.

Hannah Prentiss took a deep breath of the unusually warm autumn air blowing through her open window as she guided her green Subaru Outback along the narrow country road.

She tucked a wayward strand of blond hair behind her ear and smiled over at her friend, Lacy Minyard. "Doesn't the air smell delicious? Everything is so crisp and bright. I missed the changing seasons when I was in LA. We had some fall colors, but nothing like this. I'll never regret coming back home to Kentucky."

Lacy laughed into the breeze as she pulled her jacket around her shoulders and held on tight to the scarf she'd tied around her reddish-brown hair. "You look happier and more settled every day that you're here. I'll say it again. I'm glad you came home. I missed you."

Hannah released a happy sigh. "You know that feeling when you're absolutely sure you made the right choice, because all the pieces just fall into place?"

Lacy smiled dreamily. "That's how I felt when Neil proposed."

Hannah shook off the twinge she felt at Lacy's words. Someday, if it was God's will, she'd have that kind of love, but for now she was content to run her restaurant.

Content. That was exactly how she felt in Blackberry Valley. She had a business she loved, a community of people who welcomed her with open arms, good friends to spend her time with—including a certain handsome fire chief—and even the occasional mystery to keep things interesting. Life was good.

"I think you take the next turn up on the right," Lacy said.

"Thanks."

Lacy was playing navigator as they headed to an estate sale Hannah had seen advertised in the *Blackberry Valley Chronicle*, promising a sampling of Old Kentucky history. Hannah was always on the alert for local artifacts she could use to decorate her restaurant or the apartment she lived in above it. It was probably the residual sting of the first review of the Hot Spot, which had called the decor *generic*. Thanks to Fire Chief Liam Berthold and his grandfather, that was no longer true, but their contributions had triggered Hannah's interest in memorabilia.

She and Lacy left early in the hope of being among the first to arrive. Hannah didn't want to miss out on any treasures that might get snapped up quickly. She expected to make it back in plenty of time for the dinner rush, but she knew the Hot Spot was in good hands if they were delayed.

"You should slow down," Lacy warned. "With all these overgrown bushes it might be hard to see—"

Lacy's words were interrupted by a streak of brown and white darting into the road ahead of them. Hannah had already begun to slow, but now she slammed on the brakes and skidded to a halt scant inches from the dog that leaped up at the front of her car.

Hannah's heart pounded in her rib cage. After checking that Lacy was okay, she leaned her forehead against the steering wheel and whispered a prayer of thanks. When her pulse calmed, she lifted her head and turned to her friend. "That was a close call."

Lacy was watching the dog, who ran in circles on the road ahead, barking at them. "I think he's trying to tell us something. Like he wants us to follow him."

"I think you're right," Hannah said slowly. "Are you game?"

"We'd better. He risked his life to get our attention."

Hannah eased up on the brake and let the car inch forward. "Okay, pup. Lead the way."

They followed the dog around the turn they'd been planning to take anyway, right where the bright red ESTATE SALE SATURDAY sign marked the entrance to a rutted dirt road. *Saturday* had been crossed out and replaced with TODAY.

Hannah was grateful for the excellent suspension on her car. Based on its condition, this road wasn't frequently traveled. That didn't bother the dog though. He raced ahead, glancing back every so often to make sure they were behind him. Still wary from the near miss and not wanting to risk damaging her car, Hannah kept a slow and steady pace.

A few minutes later, she saw a large yellow farmhouse off to the right, and then the lane ended in a wide-open yard with a barn directly ahead. The dog ran straight to the barn and pranced impatiently as he waited for Hannah to park.

Lacy glanced from the dog and barn to her friend. "I guess this is the place. And he seems friendly enough."

Bright red-and-yellow banners advertising the estate sale were draped across the entry to the barn, and the barking dog made it clear that was the way he wanted them to go.

Hannah and Lacy climbed from the car and made their way to the wide barn doors. The dog seemed measurably calmer now that they were there, and he came up to them, tail wagging as he nuzzled Hannah's jean-clad legs. She ran her hand through his soft fur and felt a collar. He was healthy and clearly well-cared for, but when she slipped her hand beneath the leather band, he tugged free and nudged her forward. Obviously, he was still eager for them to keep moving.

"Hello?" Hannah called as she stepped out of the sunshine and into the dim interior of the barn. Near the entrance, dust motes drifted in the air above stacked bales of hay. Ahead, an aisle separated two rows of stalls, but the space between yawned wide and empty. "Is anyone here?"

"Help. Back here." The call was barely audible.

The dog barked again before dashing ahead.

Hannah and Lacy exchanged glances of amazement. "We're coming," Lacy called. "Keep talking if you can, so we can follow the sound of your voice."

"Or we can just listen for the dog," Hannah added with a smile as he continued to bark excitedly.

"I'm behind the stalls, back by the tack room."

The voice sounded relieved, and Hannah shared the feeling. What a good thing it was that they'd chosen to follow the dog. Lacy hurried down the aisle between the rows of empty stalls, but Hannah had to force herself to keep moving. Her ten-year-old self would have been starry-eyed and daydreaming about all these stalls filled with horses, and to be truthful, her adult self was inclined to do the same. But someone needed their help. She hurried to catch up with Lacy.

"Over here." An arm waved in the air, and Hannah hurried forward to find a young woman lying on the scattered hay.

Lacy knelt beside her. "Are you badly hurt? Do we need to call an ambulance?"

"No, I think I'll be okay once I get some ice on my ankle. I just can't get free."

Hannah could see her leg trapped beneath a large box. A stepladder rested on its side a short distance away. "What happened?" she asked as she struggled to lift the heavy box.

"I was nearly done setting up the sale when I saw that box on a shelf above the door inside the tack room. I could see some sort of trophy sticking out, so I decided to take it down to find out what was inside. I got my hand on it, but then I lost my footing. When I grabbed at the edge, it tumbled down and knocked me off the ladder." She made a face as she gestured to her leg. "Easy to see in hindsight that it was foolish to do it on my own. I'm Sylvia Parsons," she added. "How did you find me? Are you just early for the sale?"

Hannah and Lacy both introduced themselves. "Your dog came and got us," Hannah added. "He ran all the way out to the road. I guess he didn't exactly flag us down, but he sure got our attention."

The woman's jaw dropped in surprise. "He did all that?"

"He did," Lacy replied. "Nearly got himself killed running in front of the car. Lucky for him my friend here has had plenty of practice driving in LA traffic and was able to stop short. He must really love you."

The woman shrugged. "He's not mine. I never saw him before today. He was nosing around the barn all morning while I worked on setting up for the sale. I didn't see him after I fell. Now I know why. He went to get help."

"You must have been so scared," Lacy said, giving Sylvia's hand a gentle squeeze.

"I wasn't too worried. I figured someone would show up for the sale sooner or later." She shrugged. "And if not, I trusted God would provide."

Lacy laughed. "I guess He provided via a four-legged creature. I wonder what your rescuer's name is."

"He has a collar," Hannah chimed in. "I was able to grasp it earlier, but he managed to pull away before I could see if there was a tag."

"There isn't," Sylvia said. "I checked that when he came to visit me. Maybe it broke off and got lost. I wonder where he came from. He must belong to someone, given how friendly and healthy he is."

While they talked, Hannah had pulled a hay bale closer. Now they knelt behind Sylvia, one on either side, and helped to lift her until she could balance on her good foot. With Hannah and Lacy supporting her, she managed to hop over and settle on the hay.

"I can take a look at your ankle if you want," Lacy offered. "I live on a farm and have tended to more than my share of injuries. Mostly on goats and horses, of course, but some humans too." She chuckled.

Sylvia nodded. "Thank you. It might be worse than I thought. There should be some ice in the house, since the electricity is still on. I hate to ask, but—"

"Say no more," Hannah interrupted. "I'll grab the first aid kit from my car and then go find some ice. Is there someone we can call for you?"

Sylvia shook her head. "I'm just here to supervise the estate sale for my firm. I'm staying at the Blackberry Inn. I don't know anyone in town."

"Well, now you know us," Hannah reassured her. "Don't you worry."

Hannah dashed out to her car for the first aid kit before heading to the house. It felt odd walking into someone else's home, even though she knew the owners were no longer there. It was an estate sale, after all. As she glanced around the beautifully kept rooms, she couldn't help but wonder about the people who'd once made this their home. Who had they been? Why was no one left?

Hannah opened the freezer, and the burst of cold air cooled her curiosity enough that she could laugh at herself. Coming back to Blackberry Valley had not only allowed the business side of her personality to emerge, but the instinct that had made her love mysteries seemed to be thriving here too. She was finding something new to investigate every time she turned around. She had to admit that it was sure making her life here an adventure.

By the time Hannah returned with ice, Lacy had pronounced Sylvia's ankle badly bruised. They set her up by the makeshift cash register

and volunteered to help however they could. Hannah called the Hot Spot and explained the situation to Elaine Wilby. Her capable hostess promised to take over if she wasn't back by dinner.

Hannah had already hung up before it dawned on her that Elaine might know the people who'd left this estate. Her family had owned the King farm in the valley for more than a hundred years. She'd have to remember to ask her. Maybe she would even know who owned the dog.

People were beginning to trickle into the barn by then, eager to search for treasure. Remembering the box they'd left on the ground, Hannah hurried back to move it out of the way. The trophy that had caught Sylvia's eye had fallen out onto the ground. Hannah picked it up, and a thrill went through her as she held the golden cup. It was a first-place trophy for a horse race. For a moment she was ten again and dreaming of riding. She'd had a few lessons as a child and had read every horse book on the Blackberry Valley Public Library shelves. She smiled, remembering those happy days.

A peek in the box revealed another trophy and racing memorabilia. On a whim, she dragged the box over to ask Sylvia if she could purchase the contents. She'd come for artifacts for the Hot Spot after all. These weren't quite on theme for the converted firehouse, but she couldn't resist.

Once her purchase was settled, Hannah shoved the box under a table against the wall and got to work. She and Lacy were soon caught up in the excitement of the estate sale. By midafternoon, when the flow of customers dwindled, they were all exhausted. Lacy flopped down on a hay bale beside Sylvia, but Hannah had something else in mind.

"Sylvia, that box that fell on you—should we look at it together? I've been dying of curiosity all day to know what I bought."

"Let's," Sylvia agreed. "Better be something good to make up for all the trouble it's caused."

Hannah got down on her knees and tugged the box from under the table. The dog, who had vanished for most of the day, came up beside her and sniffed at the cardboard. "What do you think, pup? Is there something good inside?"

The dog yipped, and the three women burst into laughter.

Hannah settled cross-legged on the hay and opened the box. The first thing she pulled out was the golden trophy she'd set on top. "I'll bet this is what made the box topple over on you. It's really heavy." She hoisted the trophy so Sylvia could see.

Sylvia squinted and read the label out loud. "'First Place, Kentucky's Angel, April 23, 1962.' I wonder who that was. Or rather, whose horse."

Hannah set the trophy aside and pulled out another topped with a golden horse. "This one's for Kentucky's Angel too, from a year earlier." She dug back into the box, removing an assortment of ribbons, racing programs, and finally, at the bottom, a photo album with *Kentucky's Angel* embossed on the front. Hannah flipped the book open and found page after page of dried flowers. "Whoa. These look like they're from the garlands that get draped over the first-place horses, like in the Kentucky Derby."

"That's a lot of wins." Lacy took out her phone, tapped on the screen a few times, and let out a low whistle. "I haven't read the whole thing, but listen to this. 'Police have yet to uncover clues as to the whereabouts of Kentucky's Angel or her jockey, Mickey Dawes.

The pair disappeared on the eve of what was expected to be the champion filly's run for the roses.'"

Sylvia gasped, and Hannah sank back against the box, gazing at the memorabilia strewn before her. The dog nudged her leg, and Hannah smiled. "Sounds like we have two new mysteries to solve. Who owns this dog?" She patted the pup then lifted the trophy. "And what happened to Kentucky's Angel and Mickey Dawes?"

Loved *Mysteries of Blackberry Valley?*
Check out some other Guideposts mystery series!

Whistle Stop Café Mysteries

Join best friends Debbie Albright and Janet Shaw as they step out in faith to open the Whistle Stop Café inside the historic train depot in Dennison, Ohio. During WWII, the depot's canteen workers offered doughnuts, sandwiches, and a heap of gratitude to thousands of soldiers on their way to war via troop-transport trains. Our sleuths soon find themselves on track to solve baffling mysteries—both past and present. Come along for the ride for stories of honor, duty to God and country, and of course fun, family, and friends!

Under the Apple Tree
As Time Goes By
We'll Meet Again
Till Then
I'll Be Seeing You
Fools Rush In
Let It Snow
Accentuate the Positive
For Sentimental Reasons

That's My Baby
A String of Pearls
Somewhere Over the Rainbow
Down Forget-Me-Not Lane
Set the World on Fire
When You Wish Upon a Star
Rumors Are Flying
Here We Go Again
Stairway to the Stars
Winter Weather
Wait Till the Sun Shines
Now You're in My Arms
Sooner or Later
Apple Blossom Time
My Dreams Are Getting Better

Secrets from Grandma's Attic

Life is recorded not only in decades or years, but in events and memories that form the fabric of our being. Follow Tracy Doyle, Amy Allen, and Robin Davisson, the granddaughters of the recently deceased centenarian, Pearl Allen, as they explore the treasures found in the attic of Grandma Pearl's Victorian home, nestled near the banks of the Mississippi in Canton, Missouri. Not only do Pearl's descendants uncover a long-buried mystery at every attic exploration, they also discover their grandmother's legacy of deep, abiding faith, which has shaped and guided their family through the years. These uncovered Secrets from Grandma's Attic reveal stories of faith, redemption, and second chances that capture your heart long after you turn the last page.

History Lost and Found
The Art of Deception
Testament to a Patriot
Buttoned Up
Pearl of Great Price
Hidden Riches
Movers and Shakers
The Eye of the Cat
Refined by Fire

The Prince and the Popper
Something Shady
Duel Threat
A Royal Tea
The Heart of a Hero
Fractured Beauty
A Shadowy Past
In Its Time
Nothing Gold Can Stay
The Cameo Clue
Veiled Intentions
Turn Back the Dial
A Marathon of Kindness
A Thief in the Night
Coming Home

Savannah Secrets

Welcome to Savannah, Georgia, a picture-perfect Southern city known for its manicured parks, moss-covered oaks, and antebellum architecture. Walk down one of the cobblestone streets, and you'll come upon Magnolia Investigations. It is here where two friends have joined forces to unravel some of Savannah's deepest secrets. Tag along as clues are exposed, red herrings discarded, and thrilling surprises revealed. Find inspiration in the special bond between Meredith Bellefontaine and Julia Foley. Cheer the friends on as they listen to their hearts and rely on their faith to solve each new case that comes their way.

The Hidden Gate
A Fallen Petal
Double Trouble
Whispering Bells
Where Time Stood Still
The Weight of Years
Willful Transgressions
Season's Meetings
Southern Fried Secrets
The Greatest of These
Patterns of Deception

The Waving Girl
Beneath a Dragon Moon
Garden Variety Crimes
Meant for Good
A Bone to Pick
Honeybees & Legacies
True Grits
Sapphire Secret
Jingle Bell Heist
Buried Secrets
A Puzzle of Pearls
Facing the Facts
Resurrecting Trouble
Forever and a Day

A Note from the Editors

We hope you enjoyed another exciting volume in the Mysteries of Blackberry Valley series, published by Guideposts. For over seventy-five years, Guideposts, a nonprofit organization, has been driven by a vision of a world filled with hope. We aspire to be the voice of a trusted friend, a friend who makes you feel more hopeful and connected.

By making a purchase from Guideposts, you join our community in touching millions of lives, inspiring them to believe that all things are possible through faith, hope, and prayer. Your continued support allows us to provide uplifting resources to those in need. Whether through our communities, websites, apps, or publications, we inspire our audiences, bring them together, and comfort, uplift, entertain, and guide them. Visit us at guideposts.org to learn more.

We would love to hear from you. Write us at Guideposts, P.O. Box 5815, Harlan, Iowa 51593 or call us at (800) 932-2145. Did you love *Out of the Depths*? Leave a review for this product on guideposts.org/shop. Your feedback helps others in our community find relevant products.